BLOOD and WATER

Éilís Ní Dhuibhne

Attic Press, Dublin.

To my beloved Bo

Contents

The Postmen's Strike

MATILDA STRETCHED, jumped out of bed, and walked over to the window. The sun danced in irregular lines on the grass. A bird sang in the single tree. Spring had come to Denmark at last.

Matilda put on the coffee and went into the shower. She turned the water on as strongly as possible, and used more bubble-bath than was necessary. She wanted to smell extra-sweet, on the first day of spring. When she came out of the bathroom, trailing a large purple towel, she was humming a little tune. She had learned it in Ireland long ago, from the Walton's Show on Saturday afternoon. 'Deep in Canadian woods we met' was the first and the only line she knew. She hummed for the last three lines of each verse, but at the beginning of each she sang: 'Deep in Canadian woods we met.' These words had always fascinated Matilda. They had the power to conjure up two different pictures in her imagination. The first was of a member of the Canadian Mounted Police colliding with an exiled Irish Rebel in the middle of a huge pine forest — perhaps Sean Ó Duibhir an Gleanna, who liked that sort of background. The second picture was also of a Canadian Mounted Policeman, and also set in a pine forest, but this time he ran into an Irish milkmaid. What else could those words possibly mean? Matilda danced around the floor, humming, drying, and wondering. While thus occupied, she heard a thud from the hall. The post. They say you can tell a lot about a person from the way they react to the sound of the postman. Matilda always reacted in the same way: she dropped everything and flew to the mat. It was as if she were afraid he would come back and take the letters away again if she didn't pick them up one second after they arrived. In fact she had never experimented to see. No letter had ever lain on Matilda's mat for more than one second after it had been dropped there. The four times she had been away from her flat on holiday during the past ten years were periods when no post had come anyhow. There were many such interludes in Matilda's life. She had a few friends in Europe and America who sent a card or a letter now and then, but for the most part her post consisted of official correspondence. Even this afforded Matilda, who was of a cheerful disposition and easily pleased, some pleasure.

Today, one envelope lay on the mat. It bore a strange stamp, and the postmark read 'Ireland'. Matilda stared at it in astonishment. She had not had a letter from Ireland in nine and a half years. Immediately after she had left that country, ten years before, she had enjoyed a regular correspondence with her parents, siblings, husband, and literate child. But six months later, the postal workers in Ireland had gone on strike. Telecommunications also became affected, and soon it was apparent that other strikes, such as airline and shipping, were on. Nobody left the country and nobody from outside could visit it. Not that many tried: as soon as the Bord Fáilte campaigns died down, most people, including Irish emigrants, seemed to forget that the place existed. After two years, Matilda noticed that the European maps no longer marked the position of her native country. The EEC stopped referring to Ireland as a member, and Greece reigned uncontested in the slot reserved for the country which receives most and contributes least. After the official disappearance of Ireland, Matilda rarely thought of it, except when a snatch of an old song or a St Patrick's Day meeting of the Copenhagen Irish Society recalled it suddenly to mind.

She stood in the hall, shivering with apprehension and cold, since the towel had slipped down her back and it was chilly for the time of year. She opened the envelope. The single sheet was handwritten. The hand was faintly familiar, but the address and signature were not.

Ailesbury Palace,
Ballsbridge.
22 March, 1999.

My old jewel,

Hoping this finds you as it leaves me and the care? That is, well. The boys are doing fine. Things is now come to pass in Ireland where we can write letters again. The strike is over, thanks be to ____ . It was a terrible nuisance. Funny we managed all the same. The post office workers have got ten per cent. Not what they were after but it's better than nothing. Aer Lingus are back too, from this Friday. People are saying the planes are not safe, because foreigners think they're UFO's. But personally I think that's just old guff. So I'll be in Copenhagen next Wednesday, if all goes well. It'll be marvellous to have you home, all the same. I was never much of a hand at the old cooking.

Your own shegouhska

Rashers

P.S. I resigned from my job in the Department of External Affairs and am now employed as a Public Poet.

Rashers! It must be Michael, using a new name. Matilda went into the living-room and sank into her good armchair. Michael! He sounded crazy. Ireland, too, probably had gone to the dogs. Left on its own, of course, what could you expect? Wednesday, if all goes well!

Matilda took a mouthful of coffee, and then suddenly choked on it, at the thought of Michael against the backdrop of the new Copenhagen Airport. 'Deep in Canadian Woods We Met'! Wednesday. She began to calculate rapidly. Was it possible to change address, job, even town of residence, before Wednesday? The answer came effortlessly: no. There was not a hope of it. If there were, would it be worth it? The answer came slowly. Well, maybe, probably, and considering what Michael had been like ten years ago when he had not been called Rashers and had a respectable job as a Third Sec., yes. Then again, it might be interesting, and certainly it would be amusing, to find out what exactly had been going on in the Old Sod, as the Copenhagen Irish Society President called it, during the long period of isolation. And, despite what Rashers clearly imagined, there was no obligation to return. A word with Matilda's lawyer would set him straight on that point, if necessary. Probably there was no such thing as divorce in Ireland as yet, but ten years separation was grounds for something. Even if it had been her fault originally, since it was she who had insisted on coming to Copenhagen to teach Old Irish, when she really ought to have stayed at home and looked after her husband and family. Still, in a way that had been a mutual decision: they both had known her career was being frustrated by Michael's: he was to be posted to the worst mission in the world, newly opened in Uganda, a year after Matilda's trip to Copenhagen. Matilda had promised to join him without protest, if she only had one year of freedom in which to develop her own interests. She would never get the chance to teach Old Irish in Uganda. It was just not the sort of subject the Third World was interested in.

Matilda went to the sideboard and took out a bar of chocolate. She kept it there for visitors. Alcohol was practically unobtainable in Denmark in 1999: citizens were rationed to one litre of spirits per year. Feeling guilty about putting on weight, Matilda sat in the armchair and gnawed off chunks of the delicious stuff. She speculated idly about her use of chocolate as a release in moments of stress and indecision: probably it would be useless as an aid to relaxation if it were not a taboo-food.

Wednesday morning. 11 a.m., Kastrup Airport. Matilda wore a white raincoat and a dark green scarf. Her body exuded the light foliate perfume without which she felt positively naked. People glanced at her appreciatively: she cut an elegant figure, etched against the nondescript but expensive background of the Arrivals Hall.

She waited patiently: the Dublin flight had been delayed forty minutes, owing to take-off difficulties. Some things do not change, thought Matilda, lighting a cigarette and restraining an impulse to tap her small leather-shod foot against the hard floor. A middle-aged man with a head like a boiled egg came and asked her for a match. She offered him her lighter, unsmilingly. He thanked her with indelicate warmth, and stood two steps away, smoking a fat cigar. Matilda then began to tap her toe, just loud enough to be audible to him.

Finally, the flight arrived. Matilda felt nervous. She lit another cigarette, and sat down on a seat placed a short distance from the gate from which Michael would eventually emerge. Would they recognise one another? What would he look like now? What had he looked like ten years ago? A number of images were stored in the back of her mind: Michael in shorts going to play badminton; Michael going to work in blue jeans and a white shirt and tie; Michael going to bed in striped pyjamas.

She had no clear picture of Michael's face. Well, it didn't matter: it would look different now anyhow. And she, she must have changed. Years of living in Copenhagen had turned her into a slim elegant creature, quite unlike the dumpy motherly figure she had been when last in Dublin. He wouldn't know her! How would he react? How would she react? Would she shiver? Take fright and run off or be unaccountably happy in an indescribably sweet and lovely way?

People began to file through the gate in dribs and drabs until eventually there he stood, quite unmistakably. He was carrying a small suitcase and a briefcase, and, Matilda noted approvingly, a plastic bag which, she hoped, contained a tiny supply of whiskey and some cigarettes. His eyes had not changed one bit: they were wide and brown, and they darted curiously about. It was they that gave him away. Otherwise he bore no resemblance to the old Michael. He had shaved his beard and moustache. His sallow skin glistened with health and aftershave. He had become conservative in his dress, to an extent which was truly remarkable: without looking exactly like a dandy of the turn of the century, he successfully conveyed the impression of being ideologically sympathetic with say, Oscar Wilde or Jack London. His whole appearance, in short, thought Matilda, as she approached him with a carefully confident gait, had nothing in common with that of the old Michael except its slight absurdity.

He recognised Matilda as soon as he caught sight of her.

'Darling, is it really you?' he asked. His accent had an Anglo-Irish tinge, very odd when one considered the definite Hiberno-Irish flavour of his letter. He did not sound the 'r' in darling, and the 'ea' in really he pronounced as 'ay'.

'Yes, Michael. Or, should I call you "Rashers"?'

Matilda had difficulty in letting go of the last word without an accompanying giggle. But, for the second time in an hour, she suppressed a natural urge, and choked instead.

'No, no, no. Not at all, not at all. Purely a professional title. Only a nom-de-plume. Merely for amusement. Rather a catchy little appellation, isn't it, my dear?'

Michael chuckled. Matilda's covergirl face preserved its 'normal' pose, of bland dignity. She allowed her long grey eyes to express neither alarm nor amusement: it was too early in the day to take any definite line of action. The new Michael might be an eccentric genius, or he might be an idiot (like the old Michael). She should not make up her mind on a moment's acquaintance.

'I can see that it might be effective in certain types of business.'

'I am not a pork butcher, you know!'

Michael laughed. Matilda's mouth formed itself into a smile. She would not make up her mind on two moments' acquaintance either. But . . .

'How long do you plan to stay?' she asked casually, guiding him in the direction of the bar.

'Mm. Two weeks is as long as I can manage, I'm afraid. Very busy at the moment, you know, in Ireland. We are frankly up to our eyes.'

His tone suggested that Ireland was his personal office.

'You must tell me all about it. About Ireland, that is. I . . . we . . . know nothing. I hardly know where to begin.'

'There's a lot I want to find out about, too, kittens!'

Matilda blenched. She couldn't prevent it. It made her feel sick to hear him use the pet-name he had invented, according to himself, when they were both little more than twenty. Michael had not learned a sense of discretion during the ten years of absence, whatever else he had learned.

'Yes. Would you like to have a drink here? Or shall we hurry home?'

'Oh, we could have a small one, I think!'

Wondering if he knew that it would have to be a small strawberry yoghurt or a lemon juice, Matilda led him into the bar and called the waiter.

'Drinking laws have become rather tight here in the past while,' she explained to Michael. She felt she had one up on him: for some reason she was proud to live in a country with such a superior moral law.

'That's fine with me. I've been in the Pioneers for the past seven years.'

'You still have the Pioneers?' Matilda injected the question with no more than a dash of polite curiosity.

'Pioneers, Legion of Mary, Vincent de Paul; you name it, it's been revived and is flourishing in the new Ireland.'

Matilda recrossed her legs. The artificial air of the bar was making her feel itchy.

'Do you all speak Irish?'

'Bless your dear heart, no. Nobody speaks Irish. Nobody even knows Irish. It is a pagan language, with anarchic undertones in every aspiration. It's been unofficially banned since 1994.'

Michael spoke with an authoritative air which Matilda found at least as irritating as the unnatural oxygen which the Danish airline forced its customers to breathe, on land as well as in the air.

'I still teach Old Irish here.'

'How extraordinary!'

She was accustomed to defending herself against this sort of opinion.

'It's no more extraordinary than teaching Latin.'

'It is much more extraordinary than teaching Latin, and you know it.'

'Oh, the Romans and all that! We approach it from a socio-linguistic point of view. Nothing more. No value judgements are allowed.'

Matilda did not particularly wish to get involved in a tedious academic quibble with her ex-husband, or husband, or whatever he was. But academic quibbling was preferable to 'kittens' conversation.

'How can you approach it from a socio-linguistic point of view, when nothing is known about the society that spoke it, or how they spoke, or whether they spoke?'

Matilda could have explained that she was adept at

approaching 'it' from whatever point of view fashion dictated. For one prolonged period, when the Christian Democrats had been in power, she had approached it from a rigidly fascist viewpoint. Her essay, 'Maeve: an Irish precursor of Thatcher' had won her no small fame in Copenhagen's intellectual circles at that time. Later when the Christian Democrats were replaced by the Socialists (Left), owing to a new rise in the cost of petrol and the simultaneous although unconnected leaking of a reactor in a nuclear power station outside Aarhus which threatened all animal life within a radius of ten miles with extinction, she had been advised to change her approach: she revised her textbooks, and taught her student(s) to interpret all Old Irish literature as an expression of repressed communist ideals on the part of the ancient Gael.

'We know exactly what the society was like and we know exactly how they spoke. You are naturally out of touch with modern research on Ireland. If you care to read my latest work, "Marxist Dialectic in the Book of the Dun Cow", you will be brought up to date.'

Michael's eyes flashed.

'I am completely up to date, thank you. Irish researchers are now the experts on Ireland, incredible though this may seem. And we have discovered through years of patient scholarship that there was no Book of the Dun Cow. Or no Old Irish or Middle Irish and even no Book of Kells. And no High Crosses or Round Towers or Saints or Scholars, or Scribes or Bards or Harpists or Harps. Or Penal Days or Mass Rocks or Famines or Tally Sticks. Or 1798 or 1916. Or anything commonly masquerading under the title of Irish History. We have rewritten it.'

This trenchantly-delivered manifesto did not disturb Matilda in the least. She had seen histories rewritten time and again during her ten years at the University of Copenhagen.

'Indeed?' she asked, although she was not desperately interested.

'Yes. We have discovered that the Irish are simply an offshoot of the English. There were no Irish people as such before the island was settled by the English in the sixteenth century. We are all the direct descendants of the English nobility of the Renaissance period.'

'Indeed?' asked Matilda again, taking a draught of yoghurt and hoping the answer would not be too long.

'Yes, indeed, to be sure, and really and truly. And as true as I'm sitting here. We are the English as the English were before they got ruined by industrialisation and that awful coal-dust. We are the English who ruled the waves and invented the spinning jenny.'

'But not the English who span with it?'

'No, definitely not. Damned trade unionists. Social Welfare sheep.'

Matilda laughed one of her sympathetic laughs at Michael. Relaxing in his chair, his loose bow-tie flopping out over his grey jacket, his finger-nails long and clean, he was not altogether unattractive.

'Perhaps we ought to move along now? The traffic tends to get heavy after one. The great going-home, you know.'

'Certainly. Delighted. I can't wait to see your home, need I tell you? I have wondered so often how you lived, here, alone!'

Matilda wished she had a Danish husband and three children, just to show him how silly his way of thinking was.

'It has been some time, hasn't it?'

She glided along in front of him, her silk blouse swishing against the lining of her coat. She was aware of the effect she was making, on Michael and on the other onlookers, ranged around the yoghurt bar. Her satisfaction with that caused her to experience a rush of self-confidence. She felt sure she would solve this Irish question without serious difficulty.

Michael was charmed by Matilda's flat.

'It is perfectly charming,' he kept murmuring to himself, as he examined the vague but safe water-colours and the natural colourless furniture.

Matilda tried to recall their old house in Dublin. She remembered it as being reasonably habitable. But if Michael's reaction to her very modest apartment was genuine, what could his own home be like?

'You still live on Firhouse Green?'

She knew he did not.

'No, no. We moved a few years ago. In to Ballsbridge. I've got a state house, of course. A man in my position. . .'

'Of course.' Matilda took four glasses from the sideboard. And, on second thoughts, a half-consumed bar of chocolate.

'It used to be the German Embassy. Our house. When we broke off diplomatic relations with the world, we had to do something with the embassies.'

'So you distributed them among public officials?'

'We distributed them amongst ourselves. Ex-diplomats. But, yes, in a manner of speaking, you are right. Because we all became public officials, of one kind or another. Except for those who were incapable of it, owing to physical or mental deficiencies.'

Matilda poured two glasses of milk.

'And you are now a . . . Public Poet, didn't you say ?'

'Yes, indeed. I am Chief Poet of the New Ireland. We have tried to make use of the natural talents of our people. Every five years, every man, woman and child, and household pet, in the New Ireland, undergoes a test to determine his or her or its natural aptitudes. According to the results of these tests, state employment is allocated to the various individuals.'

'So all employment is nationalised?'

'Oh, yes.' Michael raised his glass to his mouth and sipped some milk. He went blue in the face.

'Pasteurised?' he spluttered.

'I suppose so.'

'Plorsoon!' He wiped his mouth with a red handkerchief.

Matilda did not inquire into the meaning of the term, and its etymology she would rather work out for herself.

'What sort of work do people mainly do?'

'Many people are food-providers. They plant potatoes and milk cows. The entire Central Plain, which now includes a substantial portion of Ulster, is one vast dairy and potato land. The coastal zones are inhabited by proper people. As it happens, many have a natural aptitude for poetics. They work for me. They lie in the dark and compose epic ballads in Hiberno-English, which we hope to export to the United States as soon as we open our doors to the international market once more. Other people, quite a lot, have a natural aptitude for nothing except talking. They sit around peat-fires all day and all night, talking their heads off. They are not productive but they are happy.'

'What language do you speak?'

'Hiberno-English. Everything must be said and written in Hiberno-English. That is the law.' Michael raised his eyebrows so that his forehead wrinkled up like a prune, and said confidentially: 'I must say, it's a hell of a relief to be able to take a break from the damned language. I have no natural aptitude for it myself: it has been uphill work.'

Matilda scrutinised him closely, and summed him up. He had changed completely. His voice was different. He spoke without that hesitation-which-was-not-quite-a-stammer which had hallmarked his oral expression in earlier days. Then, he had always seemed to be apologising for what he said, although that was so innocuous that his small, usually captive audience found it spent most of the time asking silently 'Why?' Matilda, his most faithful listener, frequently found at the end of one of his boring monologues on radical politics or the oil crisis that she had not absorbed one word of sense, so busy had her psycho-analytic faculties been during the course of the awful experience. The new Michael, alias Rashers, Public Poet in Chief of the New Ireland, was anything but apologetic. Sitting opposite Matilda, on the most comfortable chair in the room which he had selected for himself, he stared her straight in the eye. His words rang out. He impressed her with his self-assurance, which she feared might be stronger even than her own. The old Michael had been in a continuous state of dither. The new Michael knew what he was about. It was as if he had required a setting as strange and irrational as himself in order to flower. The New Ireland had been created by the likes of Michael for the likes of Michael: the world, including Matilda, might find it hard to fathom, but . . .

'There you are,' said Matilda.

'Yes,' said Michael, without a trace of that hesitation-which-was-not-quite-a-stammer, and added, with a sardonic smile: 'But I forgot one small detail. It emerged, under examination, that a small proportion of Irishmen showed an extraordinarily high ability in the field of science and technology. These people were all Christian Brothers. They were assigned the task of scientific research in the cause of the New Ireland, and have developed a new type of nuclear power, more efficient and stronger than any which has so far been evolved in any part of the world.'

Matilda decided not to be negative and ask how they knew this, and he went on: 'The I-Bomb was perfected two weeks ago. We have chosen this moment to release Europe, Africa, Asia and America from the isolation they have been suffering for so long, owing to the ten-year strike by the postmen, Aer Lingus, Sealink and Irish-Continental. The world has been exposed to the dangers of insularity for long enough. "No world is an island", as the Deputy-Chief Poet said in an address to the Department of Poets and Telepathists three weeks ago. The world is about to be introduced to the new master-race. Future generations will thank us for saving humanity from itself.'

In the course of this proclamation, Michael had poured himself a generous glass of whiskey, into one of the small tumblers which Matilda had suggestively placed on the table. Matilda eyed the whiskey greedily.

'Do you think I might have a little?' she asked. She wanted to celebrate the fact that she had caught a glimpse of a tiny spark of light. At the end of a long murky corridor there glowed a neon sign which possibly conveyed the message: New Michael equals Old Michael.

'Yes, of course. How clumsy of me not to have offered. How unforgivable. I ought to be shot. I ought to be hanged, drawn and quartered.'

Matilda poured herself a drink, and groped along the dark corridor towards enlightenment.

'Do you have capital punishment in the New Ireland?'

'Yes, yes, bless your heart, yes. Capital punishment and almost every kind of punishment you can think of. People are being punished right, left and centre. Especially left and centre. For the slightest offence.'

'Such as . . .' she said, with her poker-faced voice.

'Protesting against the true regime. Trying to escape. Trying to write books of a revolutionary nature. In Irish. Or Anglo-English. Or Hiberno-French. Attempting to assassinate the Theeshock, or his band of guards, or members of the real government, with home-made pikes. It hasn't been easy, I can tell you, building up the New Ireland. So many people had been contaminated by the old ideas, the old way of life. Their minds could not be reformed, to fit into the New Ireland. We had to develop a means of getting rid of them.'

The neon light shone brilliantly at the end of the corridor. Besides spelling out the obvious message, its light revealed a dark, indeterminate spot in Michael's intellect. Another prod or two and the precise nature of that spot would be known to Matilda.

'So you, that is, the New Ireland, plan a take-over of the world?'

> 'The epitaph of Emmet at last will be written
> When the rest of the world at our feet is lying smitten.'

'You wrote that?' Matilda took out her pocket handkerchief and grinned into it.

The spot was as soft as forest moss.

'When emotion swells up in an Irishman's
heart
To talk in rhymed couplets he feels he must
start.'

'You mean you do it all the time, when you're feeling a bit hot under the collar?'

' Hot under the collar' is hardly the phrase
I would have chosen to describe the ways
A master of poesie feels when he's pressed
By ignorant foreigners from east or from west
To explain the New Ireland in verse or in rhyme
Or in anything else that suggests the sublime. '

Michael was beginning to perspire.

'No, of course not. It was a very silly choice of expression. Kindly accept my apologies. I think the custom is positively charming.'

Relaxed at last, Matilda could allow herself to become contaminated by Michael's way of talking. She could well understand how the tendency to be verbose could grow on a person: gushing was fun!

'That's quite all right,' said Michael, hurt, and mopping his brow.

'Are you going to inform the People of Denmark of your plans?'

'When people first hear it they will not be
charmed.
I come all alone and I come all unarmed.
The moment for breaking the great new secret,
In my honest opinion, is not just quite yet.
When the moment is ripe, I will tell the world
all
By means of a personal telephone call.
The judicious use of our new Irish phones
Insures quick transmission without broken
bones.'

'When will the moment be ripe?' Matilda used her

Spanish-Inquisition tone.

'Well . . . it's . . . the problem is, that quite frankly, the moment is ripe. But . . .' Michael's cloak of authority was slipping rapidly from his shoulders.

'But,' Matilda used the unpunctuated, open-ended 'but'.

'But we have been forced by a new strike by the telephonists and postmen to postpone the ripe moment until a settlement is reached.'

Matilda smiled openly.

'And . . .'

'And . . . who knows? You . . . remember . . . the . . . last . . . time?'

He spoke in the Old Michael's voice, with that hesitation-which-was-not-quite-a-stammer impregnating every syllable.

'I remember, naturally. But surely the New Ireland can deal with a problem like that?'

'Well, it . . . it . . . is hard . . . to . . . explain . . . exactly. But . . . somehow . . . it . . . seems . . . impossible . . . We . . . cannot . . . do . . . a . . . thing . . . about . . . it.'

'Why did you come here, then?'

'Well . . . I . . . decided to seize . . . the opportunity . . . to . . . visit you . . . and . . . take . . . you back to the . . . the New Ireland.'

'You mean, Aer Lingus is liable to go on strike again soon?'

'It . . . could . . . happen . . . today . . . or tomorrow. The Post Office came out . . . after . . . two . . . days. Aer . . . Lingus . . . has . . . lasted . . . a . . . week. That . . . I . . . can . . . tell . . . you . . . is . . . a . . . bit . . . of . . . a . . . stretch.'

'Come on,' said Matilda, her mind acting swiftly. She pulled on her raincoat, her dark green scarf, and dabbed her ears with the foliate perfume without which she felt positively naked, in one second flat. She pulled Michael out of his chair and propelled him towards the door, grabbing his briefcase and suitcase in transit. But not his plastic bag.

'Where are we going?'

'To the airport.'

'Now?'

'We can't take any chances, can we? You want to go back to the New Ireland, don't you?'

Michael's expressive brown eyes suggested that he was not quite sure what his answer to the question would be. But he didn't get a chance to utter it. Before he could say 'Jack Robinson' he found himself fastened securely into a first-class seat on the evening flight to Dublin. It was only two seats behind that he had sat in on the way over that morning. Matilda was sitting next to him now, however, so he did not feel unhappy. They were going home to the New Ireland, together. They would build a new life there, with the two teenage children and the dog, in the old German Embassy on Ailesbury Road. With any luck, the strikes would all restart in a day or two. They would return to the good old New Life. Michael would lord it over the apprentice poets and journey poets and master poets, in the Department of Poets and Telepathy. What a vision!

He turned to Matilda, in a burst of confidentiality:

'Oh what a life we will have, my Matilda, Me and you and the dog and the childer!'

'Yes, darling, I can hardly wait,' said Matilda. She was only half-listening to Michael. Her eyes were riveted to the right hand of the second-in-command air hostess, who had promised . . .

The second-in-command air hostess raised her right hand a fraction of an inch and waved the third finger gently.

'Excuse me for one minute, darling. I've got to go to the Mná.' Matilda patted Michael's arm affectionately, and walked down the aisle towards the toilets. But instead of turning to the right, she turned to the left, and climbed out through the emergency exit, onto the runway. Two seconds later, the engines of the plane began to rev up. Within minutes the old boneshaker was mounting into the air above Kastrup. Matilda had a moment of sentimentality as she watched it hover unsteadily above the airport, looking like a crippled farmyard fowl among all the slim streamlined jets. The moment did not last for long, however. As she revved up her own little engine and pulled out of the airport carpark, her feeling was one of unadulterated relief.

Midwife to the Fairies

WE WERE LOOKING at the 'Late Late'. It wasn't much good this night, there was a fellow from Russia, a film star or an actor or something — I'd never heard tell of him — and some young one from America who was after setting up a prostitute's hotel or call-in service or something. God, what Gay wants with that kind I don't know. All done up really snazzy, mind you, like a model or a television announcer or something. And she made a mint out of it, writing a book about her experiences if you don't mind. I do have to laugh!

I don't enjoy it as much of a Friday. It was much better of a Saturday. After the day's work and getting the bit of dinner ready for myself and Joe, sure I'm barely ready to sit down when it's on. It's not as relaxing like. I don't know, I do be all het up somehow on Fridays on account of it being such a busy day at the hospital and all, with all the cuts you really have to earn your keep there nowadays!

Saturday is busy too of course — we have to go into Bray and do the bit of shopping like, and do the bit of hoovering and washing. But it's not the same, I feel that bit more relaxed, I suppose it's on account of not being at work really. Not that I'd want to change that or anything. No way. Sixteen years of being at home was more than enough for me. That's not to say, of course, that I minded it at the time. I didn't go half-cracked the way some of them do, or let on to do. Mind you, I've no belief in that pre-menstrual tension and post-natal depression and what have you. I come across it often enough, I needn't tell you, or I used to, I should say, in the course of my duty. Now with the maternity unit gone of course all that's changed. It's an ill wind, as they say. I'll say one thing for male patients, there's none of this depression carry-on with them. Of course they all think they're dying, oh dying, of sore toes and colds in the head and anything at all, but it's easier to put up with than the post-natals. I'm telling no lie.

Well, anyway, we were watching Gaybo and I was out in the kitchen wetting a cup of tea, which we like to have around ten or so of a Friday. Most nights we wait till it's nearer bedtime, but on Fridays I usually do have some little treat I get on the way home from work in The Hot Bread Shop there on the corner of Corbawn Lane, in the new shopping centre. Some little extra, a few Danish pastries or doughnuts, some little treat like that. For a change more than anything. This night I'd a few Napoleons — you know, them cream slices with icing on top.

I was only after taking out the plug when the bell went. Joe answered it of course and I could hear him talking to whoever it was and I wondered who it could be at that hour. All the stories you hear about burglars and people being murdered in their own homes . . . there was a woman over in Dalkey not six months ago, hacked to pieces at ten o'clock in the morning. God help her! . . . I do be worried. Naturally. Though I keep the chain on all the time and I think that's the most important thing. As long as you keep the chain across you're all right. Well, anyway, I could hear them talking and I didn't go out. And after a few minutes I could hear him taking the chain off and letting whoever it was in. And then Joe came in to me and he says:

'There's a fellow here looking for you, Mary. He says it's urgent.'

'What is it he wants? Sure I'm off duty now anyway, amn't I?'

I felt annoyed, I really did. The way people make use of you! You'd think there was no doctors or something. I'm supposed to be a nurse's aide, to work nine to five, Monday to Friday, except when I'm on nights. But do you think the crowd around here can get that into their heads? No way.

'I think you'd better have a word with him yourself, Mary. He says it's urgent like. He's in the hall.'

I knew of course. I knew before I seen him or heard what he had to say. And I took off my apron and ran my comb through my hair to be ready. I made up my own mind that I'd have to go out with him in the cold and the dark and miss the rest of the 'Late Late'. But I didn't let on of course.

There was a handywoman in this part of the country and she used to be called out at all times of the day and night. But one night a knock came to her door. The woman got up at once and got ready to go out. There was a man standing at the door with a mare.

He was a young fellow with black hair, hardly more than eighteen or nineteen.

'Well,' says I, 'what's your trouble?'

'It's my wife,' he said, embarrassed like. He'd already told Joe, I don't know what he had to be embarrassed about. Usually you'd get used to a thing like that. But anyway he was, or let on to be.

'She's expecting. She says it's on the way.'

'And who might you be?'

'I'm her husband.'

'I see,' says I. And I did. I didn't come down in the last shower. And with all the carry-on that goes on around here you'd want to be thick or something not to get this particular message straight away. But I didn't want to be too sure of myself. Just in case. Because, after all, you can never be too sure of anything in this life. 'And why?' says I to him then. 'Why isn't she in hospital, where she should be?'

'There isn't time,' he said, as bold as brass. See what I mean about getting used to it?

'Well,' says I then, 'closing maternity wards won't stop them having babies.' I laughed, trying to be a bit friendly like. But he didn't see the joke. So, says I, 'And where do you and your wife live?'

'We live on this side of Annamoe,' he said, 'and if you're coming we'd better be going. It's on the way, she said.'

'I'll come,' I said. What else could I say? A call like that has to be answered. My mother did it before me and her mother before her, and they never let anyone down. And my mother said that her mother had never lost a child. Not one. Her corporate works of mercy, she called it. You get indulgence. And anyway I pitied him, he was only a young fellow and he was nice-looking, too, he had a country look to him. But of course I was under no obligation, none whatever, so I said, 'Not that I should come really. I'm off duty, you know, and anyway what you need is the doctor.'

'We'd rather have you,' he said.

'Well, just this time.'

'Let's go then!'

'Hold on a minute, I'll get the keys of the car from Joe.'

'Oh, sure I'll run you down and back, don't bother about your own car.'

'Thank you very much,' I said. 'But I'd rather take my own, if it's all the same to you. I'll follow on behind you.' You can't be too careful.

So I went out to start the car. But lo and behold, it

wouldn't go! Don't ask me why, that car is nearly new. We got it last winter from Mike Byrne, my cousin that has the garage outside Greystones. There's less than thirty thousand miles on her and she was serviced only there a month before Christmas. But it must have been the cold or something. I tried, and he tried, and Joe, of course, tried, and none of us could get a budge out of her. So in the heel of the hunt I'd to go with him. Joe didn't want me to, and then he wanted to come himself, and your man . . . Sean O'Toole, he said his name was . . . said OK, OK, but come on quick. So I told Joe to get back inside to the fire and I went with him. He'd an old Cortina, a real old banger, a real farmer's car.

'Do not be afraid!' said the rider to her. 'I will bring you home to your own doorstep tomorrow morning!'

She got up behind him on the mare.

Neither of us said a word the whole way down. The engine made an awful racket, you couldn't hear a thing, and anyway he was a quiet fellow with not a lot to say for himself. All I could see were headlights, and now and then a signpost: Enniskerry, Sallygap, Glendalough. And after we turned off the main road into the mountains, there were no headlights either, and no house-lights, nothing except the black night. Annamoe is at the back of beyonds, you'd never know you were only ten miles from Bray there, it's really very remote altogether. And their house was down a lane where there was absolutely nothing to be seen at all, not a house, not even a sheep. The house you could hardly see either, actually. It was kind of buried like at the side of the road, in a kind of a hollow. You wouldn't know it was there at all until it was on top of you. Trees all around it too. He pulled up in front of a big five-bar gate and just gave an almighty honk on the horn, and I got a shock when the gate opened, just like that, the minute he honked. I never saw who did it.

But looking back now I suppose it was one of the brothers. I suppose they were waiting for him like.

It was a big place, comfortable enough, really, and he took me into the kitchen and introduced me to whoever was there. Polite enough. A big room it was, with an old black range and a huge big dresser, painted red and filled with all kinds of delph and crockery and stuff. Oh you name it! And about half a dozen people were sitting around the room, or maybe more than that. All watching the telly. The 'Late Late' was still on and your one, the call-girl one, was still on. She was talking to a priest about unemployment. And they were glued to it, the whole lot of them, what looked like the mother and father and a whole family of big grown men and women. His family or hers I didn't bother my head asking. And they weren't giving out information for nothing either. It was a funny set up, I could see that as clear as daylight, such a big crowd of them, all living together. For all the world like in 'Dallas'.

Well, there wasn't a lot of time to be lost. The mother offered me a cup of tea, I'll say that for her, and I said yes, I'd love one, and I was actually dying for a cup. I hadn't had a drop of tea since six o'clock and by this time it was after twelve. But I said I'd have a look at the patient first. So one of them, a sister I suppose it was, the youngest of them, she took me upstairs to the room where she was. The girl. Sarah. She was lying on the bed, on her own. No heat in the room, nothing.

After a while they came to a steep hill. A door opened in the side of the hill and they went in. They rode until they came to a big house and inside there were lots of people, eating and drinking. In a corner of the house there lay a woman in labour.

I didn't say a word, just put on the gloves and gave her the examination. She was the five fingers, nearly into the second stage, and she must have been feeling a good bit of pain but she didn't let on, not at all. Just lay there with her teeth gritted. She was a brave young one, I'll say that for her. The waters were gone and of course nobody had cleaned up the mess so I asked the other young one to do it, and to get a heater and a kettle of boiling water. I stayed with Sarah and the baby came just before one. A little girl. There was no trouble at all with the delivery and she seemed all right but small. I'd no way of weighing her, needless to say, but I'd be surprised if she was much more than five pounds.

'By rights she should be in an incubator,' I said to Sarah, who was sitting up smoking a cigarette, if you don't mind. She said nothing. What can you do? I washed the child . . . she was a nice little thing, God help her . . . I wrapped her in a blanket and put her in beside the mother. There was nowhere else for her. Not a cot, not even an old box. That's the way in these cases as often as not. Nobody wants to know.

I delivered the afterbirth and then I left. I couldn't wait to get back to my own bed. They'd brought me the cup of tea and all, but I didn't get time to drink it, being so busy and all. And afterwards the Missus, if that's what she was, wanted me to have a cup in the kitchen. But all I wanted then was to get out of the place. They were all so quiet and unfriendly like. Bar the mother. And even she wasn't going overboard, mind you. But the rest of them. All sitting like zombies looking at the late-night film. They gave me the creeps. I told them the child was too small, they'd have to do something about it, but they didn't let on they heard. The father, the ould fellow, that is to say, put a note in my hand . . . it was worth it from that point of view, I'll admit . . . and said, 'Thank you.' Not a word from the rest of them. Glued to the telly, as if nothing was after happening. I wanted to scream at them, really. But what could I do? Anyway the young fellow, Sean, the father as he said himself, drove me home. And that was that.

Well and good. I didn't say a word about what was after happening to anyone, excepting of course to Joe. I don't talk, it's not right. People have a right to their privacy, I always say, and with my calling you've to be very careful. But to tell the truth they were on my mind. The little girl, the little baby. I knew in my heart and soul I shouldn't have left her out there, down there in the back of beyonds, near Annamoe. She was much too tiny, she needed care. And the mother. Sarah, was on my mind as well. Mind you, she seemed to be well able to look after herself, but still and all, they weren't the friendliest crowd of people I'd ever come across. They were not.

But that was that.

Until about a week later, didn't I get the shock of my life when I opened the evening paper and saw your one, Sarah, staring out at me. Her round baby face, big head of red hair. And there was a big story about the baby. Someone was after finding it dead in a shoebox, in a kind of rubbish dump they had at the back of the house. And she was arrested, in for questioning, her and maybe Sean O'Toole as well. I'm not sure. In for questioning. I could have dropped down dead there and then.

I told Joe.

'Keep your mouth shut, woman,' he said. 'You did your job and were paid for it. This is none of your business.'

And that was sound advice. But we can't always take sound advice. If we could the world would be a different place.

The thing dragged on. It was in the papers. It was on the telly. There was questioning, and more questioning, and trials and appeals and I don't know what. The whole country was in on it.

And it was on my conscience. It kept niggling at me all the time. I couldn't sleep, I got so I couldn't eat. I was all het up about it, in a terrible state really. Depressed, that's what I was, me who was never depressed before in my life. And I'm telling no lie when I say I was on my way to the doctor for a prescription for Valium when I realised there was only one thing to do. So instead of going down to the surgery, didn't I turn on my heel and walk over to the Garda barracks instead. I went in and I got talking to the sergeant straight away. Once I told them what it was about there was no delaying. And he was very interested in all I had to say, of course, and asked me if I'd be prepared to testify and I said of course I would. Which was the truth. I wouldn't want to but I would if I had to. Once I'd gone this far, of course I would.

Well, I walked out of that Garda station a new woman. It was a great load off my chest. It was like being to confession and getting absolution for a mortal sin. Not that I've ever committed a mortler, of course. But you know what I mean. I felt relieved.

Well and good.

Well. You'll never believe what happened to me next. I was just getting back to my car when a young fellow . . . I'd seen him somewhere before, I know that, but I couldn't place him. He might have been the fellow that came for me on the night, Sean, but he didn't look quite like him. I just couldn't place him at all . . . anyway, he was standing there, right in front of the car. And I said hello, just in case I really did know him, just in case it really was him. But he said nothing. He just looked behind him to see if anyone was coming, and when he saw that the coast was clear he just pulled out a big huge knife out of his breast pocket and pointed it at my stomach. He put the heart crossways in me. And then he says, in a real low voice, like a gangster in 'Hill Street Blues' or something:

'Keep your mouth shut. Or else!'

And then he pushed a hundred pounds into my hand and he went off.

I was in bits. I could hardly drive myself home with the shock. I told Joe of course. But he didn't have a lot of sympathy for me.

'God Almighty, woman,' he said, 'what possessed you to go to the guards? You must be off your rocker. They'll be arresting you next!'

Well, I'd had my lesson. The guards called for me the next week but I said nothing. I said I knew nothing and

I'd never heard tell of them all before, the family I mean. And there was nothing they could do, nothing. The sergeant hadn't taken a statement from me, and that was his mistake and my good luck I suppose, because I don't know what would have happened to me if I'd testified. I told a priest about the lie to the guards, in confession, to a Carmelite in White Friar Street, not to any priest I know. And he said God would understand. 'You did your best, and that's all God will ask of you. He does not ask of us that we put our own lives in danger.'

There was a fair one day at Baile an Droichid. And this woman used to make market socks and used to wash them and scour them and take them to the fair and get them sold. She used to make them up in dozen bunches and sell them at so much the dozen.

And as she walked over the bridge there was a great blast of wind. And who should it be but the people of the hill, the wee folk! And she looked among them and saw among them the same man who had taken her on the mare's back to see his wife.

'How are ye all? And how is the wife?' she said.

He stood and looked at her.

'Which eye do you see me with?' he asked.

'With the right eye,' she said.

Before he said another word he raised his stick and stuck it in her eye and knocked her eye out on the road.

'You'll never see me again as long as you live,' he said.

Sometimes I do think of the baby. She was a dawny little thing, there's no two ways about it. She might have had a chance, in intensive care. But who am I to judge?

Looking

THE TELEVISION set broke down on Saturday night. No warning had been given. They were sitting there in the white armchairs when suddenly the picture fizzled away to a small circular rainbow, and then to a blank. The voices remained, persistent jets of bright frivolous argument shooting into the room. But, even though the programme had been a 'talk show' they didn't continue to listen to it. It seemed unnatural to listen to television.

The breakdown would prove significant, Margaret immediately divined. Indeed, it would blight the weekend. In the first place. Edward would become depressed at the thought of one more item in his ever-disintegrating flat having failed him. He would take it as a personal blow struck by a life which he considered to be waging a constant vendetta against him. He would feel, as he usually felt when these catastrophes occurred, that life was surely gaining ground and that the next blow would be its supreme trump. He would feel all this, and Margaret would know it, but he would tell her nothing and turn away from her. In short, he would be grumpy and that would be enough to spoil her weekend anyway.

But in the second place, she would be left physically alone and bored. Their principal shared activity was television watching. 'Dallas' and 'The Late Late Show' on Saturday night, 'The Sunday Night Feature Film' on Sundays. He supplied a running commentary as they watched. Her grandfather used to do that, she recalled, long ago in her parents' kitchen, drumming his feet against the tiles at the same time. She had hated it then and tried to freeze the old man into silence.

Now she listened and laughed at Edward, not from any motivation of politeness but because she enjoyed his patter and the sound of his voice. How much better it was than the sound of his fingers drumming against the typewriter in the study, while she sat at the kitchen table and tried to work. Typing was his other weekend activity, and one which he naturally engaged in alone.

He fiddled with the knobs on the television set for what seemed to her a very long time before accepting that the thing was simply broken, a fact which had seemed very obvious to Margaret from the outset. He suggested, in the tones of a broken man who is grinning and bearing it, that they play Scrabble and she gladly acquiesced. She was the weaker player of the two. From a sense of superiority and altruism, she played a considerate game, spreading long words across the board in order to make it accessible. He played ruthlessly. In other games, card games or dice games, he usually let her win. Perhaps he thought it was important to prove oneself at Scrabble. No, it was impossible! It might have been because of the broken television set. Anyway, he used as many triple-word scores as possible, and won by a large margin, something which pleased Margaret a little since it might make him happy, and annoyed her because she liked to win games. Then she worried. He was always so ruthless and victorious, in important things, while she was always pluralistic and defeated. Was it the difference between masculinity and femininity or activity and passivity or simply between him and her? Whatever it was, she wished the gap were narrower. She ought to win sometimes, at something, she felt.

They had survived Saturday night without television. That was a victory for both of them. At eleven, the Scrabble game was over, and they went to bed. He read 'The Song of Roland' in Old French. She turned off her lamp and fell asleep.

Early in the morning, she heard his voice murmuring beside her, like the far-off whirr of a lawnmower. Vaguely conscious of a hot projection of sun streaming through a gap in the curtains, she switched back into sub-consciousness. Her dream was suffused with light and sweat. A seaside scene flashed across her eyes. She knew it to be Brighton. She walked along a wide green park close to the water. Cotton-clad crowds milled through it, sporting sunglasses which glittered harshly and hid their souls. At the end of the park a fairground loomed: merry-go-round, ferris wheel, swings. She moved in the direction of the swings but a hand pulled her away. A white hotel, cruel and cold as only white seaside hotels can be, jutted up in front of her. A voice said: 'It's time to change.' She was pulled along towards the white concrete, filled with bleakness and despair. She still walked by the water. It wasn't green or grey or blue, but as clear as glass. She could see right down to the bottom. People were swimming underwater; men in dark suits and hats, women in coloured frocks and high-heeled shoes. One person rode a bicycle, up and down, round and round, under the water. All the people moved like fishes with blank faces and invisible strokes and they were silent as fishes. There was no noise in the dream now at all.

She awoke, properly this time. Sunlight still poured onto the foot of the bed, and the room was hot and sticky.

'Oh, you turned on the heater?'

She could see its red glow.

'I told you that an hour ago. It was so very cold. I've saved you from freezing.' His face was pale and the crow's feet around his eyes seemed to have multiplied during the night. He sniffed. A cold. She had anticipated it.

'How are you this morning?'

She leaned over and ruffled his hair. It was dark grey and soft. She loved it. Morning was her happiest time, no matter what.

'I don't know.' He lay back and directed his attention to the ceiling. His pyjamas were blue. 'I think I want to lie in bed today, and read.'

'Poor darling!'

She crawled down to the end of the bed and jumped out. The room was so narrow that there was no space at the sides. It had been built for a single bed. These were bachelor apartments. Most of the people in them were not bachelors, however, but spinsters, a fact which reflected something, something statistical, Margaret sometimes thought, not without a wince.

The living room was cold after the stuffy bedroom. The green carpet selfishly sucked in the sun. But, in the kitchen, it bounced back from the chromium-plated cooker and kettle, and danced on the walls. She stuck two pieces of bread in the toaster and began to sing. She felt like a housewife. Especially like a housewife she had seen in a film a week before. It had been a silly film, a badly disguised fantasy, in which all the women were married and thin and beautiful. They spent their mornings making toast and pouring out orange juice in sunlit kitchens, their afternoons playing tennis and complaining about their boredom. Well, they had plenty to complain about, she was sure of that. But at least they had the sun. That was a realistic detail. She remembered American kitchens herself, and they had always been filled with sun and sparkling orange juice first thing in the morning. In Ireland, sun didn't often happen, but today was an exception, and moreover, they had orange juice.

She opened a tin and mixed it with water, and then turned to the stove to make porridge. Edward always had porridge when she came to make it. It was a ritual, one of her privileges and duties. She couldn't eat it, but liked to see it boil. Today, as always, she stood and gazed into the hissing beige mess, enjoying the tiny eruptions and listening to the explosive sounds: plut, plut, plut plut! Or was it plap plap, plap plap? A fine distinction in sound existed, she knew, between different brands of oatmeal, but she had never been able to decide what the precise sound of any particular brand was.

Plop! The morning papers dropped through the letterbox. What a luxurious noise, the utter confirmation of the Sabbath! In answer, the sound of Edward springing out of bed came to her ears. She stopped staring at the porridge, reluctantly, and began to tinker with cups and plates on the table. He looked into the kitchen, his head sticking out of the dark pyjamas, pale and smiling.

'I'll get up, after all,' he said, rather cheerfully. She said: 'Ah!' and continued to play with the cups. He had not put on his spectacles. She had fallen in love with him in his spectacles, and he never attracted her without them.

They read as they ate, and went on reading for an hour or more afterwards. It was a silent period during which only the crackle of folding newspaper broke the vacuum of the flat. Sometimes, on Sunday mornings, he talked, and pointed out interesting snippets of news. Not today. Perhaps his cold exhausted his spare energy. She did not talk at all. She never did, unless he began. At other times, she might have resented this silence and suffered. Today, she accepted it as an inevitable contribution to the mood of the weekend. As it happened, her mind was silent, too, and held only blank, white impressions.

After lunch, Edward retired to bed, looking relieved to escape into the small stuffy room. Tired of cooking and of washing up without any encouragement, she sat down in an armchair again and opened a book. The sun had crept around to the corner of the flat, and there was only one sickly yellow line dividing the carpet, at an oblique angle. It had an old autumnal quality, even though it was spring. She felt a slight nausea. The day was slipping away, barren as autumn. Unbearable.

'I think I'll go for a walk,' she told Edward. He was sitting up, reading P.G. Wodehouse with apparent glee. He looked hurt, as she had known he would, but he said: 'All right.' She went outside. The air was morning-like, not at all what it had been in the flat. Instead of walking, she took her bicycle, and cycled down the road towards Blackrock. The sea spread out below her, navy blue and vital. It was a cold day, despite the sun, and when she looked back at the Dublin Mountains they were capped with snow. April was filled with incongruities, usually expected but still stimulating when they occurred. As she cycled, she grew warm, and approaching Dun Laoghaire she could not remember what cold was.

The motion of cycling freed her physically, and, as her blood began to circulate faster, her mind began to loosen. The air raced past her and through her: it seemed to penetrate her brain and tease it into activity. It pushed her hair against her face and into her eyes, and she was happy to have hair and be thus made aware of it.

The route she had chosen for her cycle was a lively one. From Blackrock to Dalkey, hundreds of people jogged. It was National Milk Run Day, and they jogged for charity, tripping along the footpaths in small groups. At Seapoint, canoes rode the white-tipped waves, with a tender appealing movement, and a swimmer walked down the slip into the sea — she would freeze to death if she got in.

At Dun Laoghaire, sailboats bobbed around in the bay, and at Dalkey people rode on surfboards with sails, looking like large coloured bats. It was the town of Dun Laoghaire which gave greatest cause for wonder, however. Like an anthill, it teemed with people. They walked up and down the promenade, up and down the pier, up and down the main street. They talked a little, and shouted at children, and ate oranges and chocolate. They spent long long periods standing in queues waiting to buy ice-cream. Many of them did not walk, or talk, or eat, but simply stared. They stared at the waves, at the boats, at the mailboat which was moored and would remain so for hours. They gazed at the lighthouse and at shops, and some of them even stared at Margaret, as she cycled, quickly, past.

Near the railway station, a large crowd had gathered to peer over the wall at the railway line, where workmen operated a large and noisy but by no means unusual machine. What is this life so full of care we have no time to stand and stare, far-off children's voices chanted from Margaret's past. The children had not had time to stare. But in Dun Laoghaire, everyone had too much time. They were for the most part doing nothing else. Margaret was staring herself, even as she moved past different scenes. The long finger of the pier pointed at the truth: she had been staring for years, at herself and at life and especially at Edward weaving an elaborate passage through her existence while being nevertheless in staunch command of his own. No bell-jar pinned her to barren patch of reality. Edward made few explicit demands, he used no padlocks. But she stood and stared like a big-eyed cow and never mooed. That was why she fantasised sometimes about cycling down to the end of Dun Laoghaire Pier and going on cycling down to the bottom of the sea.

The meaning of her life had been plain to her from the moment she woke up this morning, if not before. She had so often conjured up the image of her dramatic end, in the freezing cold water. She had even imagined the gasps for breath, the horror of the realisation that she would not surface, the fear of slimy eels and mackerel which scavenged always in the bay. She was a coward and would not take the final step, not now and probably never, but she would deserve it and be forced to it if she did not stop staring ineptly at foreign surfaces. The air whipped past her and into her, but she needed to be a part of that air, to be a dynamic collection of atoms in continual interaction with the world, if she were to be saved.

She cycled faster and faster, and reflected very vaguely in a deep part of her belly that perhaps she would be knocked down by a car. But when she found herself swerving towards one, just at the large grey wall of

Longford Terrace, she braked so hard that she jumped off the saddle and her breath was rammed into a hard ball in her chest. Faster and faster she cycled, thinking of herself lying in a hospital bed, in a ward with brown linoleum on the floor and pink dusty curtains on the windows. Her mother and father would be there waiting anxiously for the moment when her eyes would open. They would, at last, and she would peer up and see their old wrinkled faces. Edward's would not be there: he had said he would never visit her in hospital if she became ill, and stressed the point that she should not visit him either, if he did, something which he considered much more probable and imminent. Or would he perhaps be there? She did not know exactly which ending she would choose to this incident if she were God plotting it in a grubby little notebook in the sky above Blackrock. Or even if she were herself.

She pondered the sequel to his being present at her hospital bed or not present, as she locked her bicycle to the downpipe outside his hall door. She let herself into the flat. He was not in the living room. When she looked into his bedroom, he was lying asleep in semi-darkness. The paperback Wodehouse was upsidedown on the counterpane. She smiled over the end of the bed and crawled up beside him. He wasn't snoring. He never did snore. It was, she considered, closing her eyes and tucking herself in against his large warm body, an advantage not to be under-estimated.

Kingston Ridge

WE HAD COUSINS in London, Birmingham, Leeds and Holyoke, Massachusetts. The latter we never saw, except in photographs which they sent when they made their First Holy Communions, or graduated from high school — ostentatiously capped and gowned. These were placed, unframed apart from the white cardboard surrounds of their mounts, on the mantelpiece in the front room, where they remained until they fell down or got lost or thrown away. Occasionally, in my earliest youth, parcels of clothing were also sent from America: I had two dresses, one of silk tartan with a fake black bolero, one of brilliant blue nylon, a material not easily available in Ireland at that time. I prized them as the exotic artefacts they were. But before I was five the parcels stopped coming. Perhaps the custom of sending them died out then. Or perhaps too many cousins were arriving too regularly in Holyoke.

With our English relations contact was much more frequent. They all came every other year, and the cousin from Leeds, Diana, with her long red plaits swinging, came as often as twice annually, accompanied, needless to add, by her mum and dad, Auntie Jane and Uncle Mick. He was my father's brother, Uncle Mick, one of many Uncle Micks in our family. He worked in a coal-mine and suffered from a bronchial infection, so that at any moment he was liable to snatch a small plastic inhaler from his pocket and sniff furiously for several seconds. His head was bald and his belly rotund, and he spent a sizeable portion of every day of his holidays in Ryans, our local pub, having what he liked to refer to, with a hackneyed humour which typified his conversational style, as 'the black stuff'. Sometimes he brought it home and gave it to the non-drinking members of the family — Mother, Auntie Jane, Diana, me and my sisters. On such occasions he would pour it into delph breakfast cups and add two spoonfuls of sugar to each one. He believed literally in the advertisement for the beverage, and so did we all. Anyway, it tasted very pleasant, with the sugar.

Auntie Jane was a Londoner, and she possessed what nobody else I knew had: glamour. It was quite a different stylishness from that of Mother, dressed up on Sundays for Mass in her good red suit and straw hat, her black patent shoes with the sling-back heels. If anything, Auntie Jane's clothes were dull. Her skirts were all dark and pleated, her jumpers were plain, neutrally coloured. Her stockings — we could hardly believe it — were black. I could never understand what always made her seem so chic. Now I know what it was. She had a slender figure, an attribute possessed by women in the 1950's as a natural gift or not at all. Most women in Ireland, at least those with whom I was acquainted, were not thin and had not been taught that they ought to aspire to that condition. They ate as children ate: as much as they felt like, and often the kind of food that children ate, too. Bread and biscuits, bars of chocolate whenever they could have them. Auntie Jane was choosy. She liked chocolate all right, but she never ate potatoes, and for breakfast she had two cigarettes and a cup of tea. We did not connect her looks with her diet: that we attributed to nervousness. Auntie Jane was jittery, she had bags under her eyes, bags of tiredness, permanent fatigue. The inevitable result, we were informed, of being a working mother. Auntie Jane, like all the English aunts, had a job. She worked the night shift in a factory that made parts for telephones. That explained, to some extent, why Diana had two or three holidays abroad every year, while we, whose mother stayed at home to mind us, had none. It partly explained it, although not fully. The main reason for the anomaly was, as I realised before I was seven, that people in England were all automatically richer than people in Ireland. Wealth seemed to be as much their divine right as their elegant accents. Nature had ordained that they should have toilet bags stuffed with perfumes and powders, suitcases filled with lovely clothes, hot baths every morning. Money for boat fares, train fares, trips to the pictures. Money to throw away. Whereas we had money only for eating or keeping.

They had a price to pay for their privilege, of course. I knew this because Mother, who knew, had to know, the price of everything, often told me what it was: dirt and danger. England was a filthy risky place. There was no green grass there (I envisaged fields of concrete). There were no trees. There were no parks. What England did possess, in great abundance, were murderers. They lurked in the grim streets, lying in wait for children whose mothers were out working. They dragged them off with promises of sweets, to woods (what woods?), where they chopped them to bits, put them in bags, sold them to cafés which served them up for dinner, with chips and tomato ketchup.

Although this picture of England had certain attractions, it was not easy to reconcile it with my view of Diana and her lifestyle. To me she seemed an utterly charming person leading an eminently desirable existence. It was supposed to be a great calamity that she was an only child. But I, blessed with three sisters, could not but envy her status. The apple of her parents' eye, never slapped, seldom scolded, she was, we all said, 'spoiled rotten'. The very worst fate that could befall any child, after being an 'only', was to be given things it liked to have, to be permitted participation in adult conversations, to be accorded rights reserved in Ireland for those who had reached their legal majority, or, perhaps, the age at which they could take the mail-boat. Diana seemed to be protected by some special Acts which did not cover us. She was encouraged to express opinions, to issue requests. 'Full of old backchat', was what she was. As a result, she had a calm self-confidence which I entirely lacked. And this in itself was an enviable trait.

More significantly, she had toys and sweets and a whole wardrobe-full of the very latest in girls' clothes. She had a special toybag, transported from Leeds on every holiday, full of brightly-painted, unbroken playthings: Lego bricks, dolls that could talk and pee, giant wooden jigsaws depicting jolly scenes from Disney films, so much simpler to assemble than the jigsaws Santy left for us, prints of 'The Titanic' or 'The Mona Lisa' in five thousand miniscule pieces, most of which seemed to be lost already before one opened the box.

The school Diana went to was private, and in it there was a gymnasium where she had learned to vault a horse and a swimming-pool where she had perfected the backstroke and crawl. She also had a school-uniform, and she brought it over one year, just to give us a chance to admire it: a purple tunic and blazer, and a purple hat, a real hat, not a beret like the ones we wore to the Sisters of Mercy. There was a velvet band on the hat, in a nicely contrasting shade of pale lilac, and she had lilac knee-socks to match, rounded off by brilliant Daisy Bell shoes, a type of shoe I always coveted, but never actually got.

In short, Diana had everything. It was no wonder that her visits were both the highlights and the lowlights of our life. I always believed them to be pure blessings, however. In particular the holiday she spent with us every summer, the first fortnight in August, filled me with a sense of acute festivity. Since we had very few family outings, relying on free passes which my father sometimes got from CIE for one or two trips to unpopular towns in the midlands, like Mullingar or Roscommon, the visitors provided the only whiff of holiday atmosphere I got, except for that which filled the convent on the last day of term and that which emanated from the radio in the kitchen from June onwards:

> 'We're going on a twopenny busride
> We'll have a holiday for two!
> Look alive!
> All aboard!
> Maybe I'm dreaming, I don't know!'

Vicariously, I enjoyed busrides to Howth and Killiney, to the Zoo, to the shops in Grafton Street. And sometimes, sometimes, Auntie Jane would bring us along, and then I knew the precise pleasure of taking the train from Harcourt Street to Bray and swimming from the great drifts of grey stones which lay piled up on the beach, or of drinking a glass of orange squash in the clattering bustle of Bewleys. Maybe I'm dreaming. This didn't happen more than once on any holiday. There were so many of us, and it wasn't fair to leave anyone out. But I always hoped. I was full of hope.

Not, however, that I would ever be like Diana, ever live like her. It was as inconceivable to me that I should enjoy her material advantages as that I should actually be her. And, although we had at least one trait in common, a shared inheritance, I knew that we were elementally different. And it seemed to me then that that distinction had a lot to do with what we possessed. There was no division between what I had and what I was, and both seemed to me to be static, permanent conditions. You were fat or thin. You were bald or redhaired. You were rich or poor. My destiny was always to live in Exeter Place, to go on weekly shopping trips to Moore Street and to haul bags of fish and vegetables home along the hot streets, to wear handmedowns and never to have pocket money. That was life, and that was me. A me with whom I was not altogether discontented, but certainly not satisfied either.

The realisation that there was another kind of life, rich and more glamorous, and deliciously distant, gave me great joy. The very knowledge of its existence was delightful. And it gave me more than a little pleasure to be in the company of the favoured ones who enjoyed that existence. To stand in the back garden, under the long dining-room window, staring through the glass at Diana as she ate her tea in state at the white-clothed table, was not painful, as it should have been, but almost the opposite: Diana was, after all, kind. She would come to the window, she would press her nose against it and make funny faces, she would mouth messages: 'I'll be out after my second cup of tea!' She was fun! And to have an aunt who, though tired in a way which my mother never was, was never worried, as all Irish mothers seemed to be as a matter of course, did not arouse any envy or suspicion in me, but gave me some curious comfort. She was my aunt, Auntie Jane, after all. And some of her slenderness, and her jollity, and her carefreeness, rubbed off on me, as the smell of her cologne clung to the furniture long after she had left the house and gone back to England. She was happy, Auntie Jane. Possibly the only happy woman I knew during my childhood. Or so it seemed.

She had a gift. She could transform, by the force of her glamour and humour, an ordinary event into a festive occasion. The moment of the day which I hated most, as a rule, was the time after breakfast when I stood in front of the mirror on the kitchen wall, and had my hair 'done' by my mother. I had long hair, flowing down my back to the end of my spine, and once a day it had to be woven into tight plaits in order to survive the rigours of my existence. Diana had hair of exactly the same length, and also of the same colour and type. Like me, she never mastered the difficult art of arranging it herself. So, every morning, we would stand in front of the mirror, and our mothers would position themselves behind us. Their hands, Auntie

Jane's long and thin and Mother's tiny and plump, worked on our respective heads, freeing the sleep-rumpled plaits from their elastic bands, brushing the hair, which rippled down our backs in regular waves like chestnut rivers, dividing it into strands, six on each head, and then weaving the strands with quick skilled movements of the fingers until we both looked presentable once more. Diana's plaits were always a bit looser than mine, thick soft ropes hanging over the sloping shoulders, while mine were taut and rather close together, like two asps stretching from neck to bottom.

While they brushed and wove the hair, Auntie Jane chatted with Mother, about clothes, about children, and about looks. Diana's strong and weak points . . . she needed a little orthodontic work on her two front teeth, her skin was tending to be spotty. My hair was commented upon, my eyes which were too close set, but which were compensated for by my full mouth, a family trait shared by me and Uncle Mick and Father, but not by any of the other children. Angela's curls, Clare's long legs and short body, the colours which suited everybody best, the great new materials, nylon, rayon; the best way to wash wool: these, and many other topics, of a nature sometimes described as 'female' would be broached, while Diana and I fretted and gloried in the attention which shorter-haired children did not get. And once or twice, when restraints loosened, the great female subjects, those reserved for the lowered voice, the private cup of tea, 'run off now and play girls!', were raised at these sessions. The terrible wonderful secrets. Periods that drained you out, breasts cut off, hysterectomies . . . what do I mean, hysterectomies? . . . 'Her womb was removed' was what they would have said. These subjects, so dear to me and Diana, and so terrifying, were lightly brushed, hinted at. Mainly, however, they were not and the atmosphere at the hair-doing was gay and easy, the superficial chatter punctuated with Auntie Jane's loud laugh at every interval, and occasionally by my mother's short more hesitant chuckle.

Diana's visits brought with them pleasure and joy, and inevitably left a sour taste in their wake. Our house, which normally seemed all right, became empty and lifeless when the guests vacated it. Their presence glorified it and filled it with an easy luxury which was beyond its capabilities. For a day or two after they left, it was revealed in all its tawdriness for what it truly was: poor.

I did not want to be poor. But, although I would not have described my condition as being impoverished . . . none of us would have . . . I was aware of it as being such. Diana was largely responsible for this consciousness. Anybody comparing her condition to ours would have been forced to the same conclusion. Even I, anxious to avoid such disgraceful truths, would have felt it. But, in case I didn't, she pointed it out. 'Why haven't you got two pairs of sandals like mine?' 'Why don't you visit us in Leeds?' 'Where is your Dad's car?'

I had no answers for her. But I knew the answer, and it gave me pain. The poverty itself was not of a kind to cause any particular hardship to me, to any child. The pain I suffered from was purely psychological: thanks to Diana, I was embarrassed to be poor. It seemed a sinful and shameful state to be in. The good, the beautiful, the normal people had money. We were in the wrong, since we didn't have it. It was a fact we would have to hide, it was dirty linen. And we did hide it, at least I did, and my mother did, until it became impossible to do so.

This point was reached in the middle of the 1960's, when Ireland was about to make its great economic leap forward. Just then, perhaps before or perhaps after the point, or more likely during it, since in reality such leaps forward do not occur overnight, there was a long bus strike. My father, a conductor, went out with the rest.

The strike started early in the summer, and initially it seemed like a holiday. Having Father at home all day gave the house a gaiety which it lacked in his absence. Mother was in excellent humour: she wore her best clothes, and put on her lipstick and eye-shadow, and invented new exciting meals for us from the summer vegetables which we could buy in abundance, with Father around to help carry them home. As for us, the girls, we were allowed to change our clothes as often as we liked, and Mother was making us new dresses, with the aid of a sewing machine she had borrowed from her sister in Rathgar, Auntie Molly. She sat at the dining-room window in the sun, pulling the cotton material, white with pink stripes, through the machine, her feet pumping busily on the foot pedal, her eyes shining with concentration.

As it became apparent that the strike would last for weeks, or months, rather than the few days everyone had predicted initially, the jovial atmosphere was dissipated, and life gradually became hard as it never had been before. We got no money for sweets now at all, and we didn't even ask if we could have a shilling for the pictures on Saturdays. Dinners came to consist of potatoes, with the occasional sausage or piece of boiled mutton. And, although it did not seem to be a logical consequence of a cash shortage, the house became dirty and untidy, and we never had decent clothes, except, of course, for Mass on Sundays. Mother gave up on the new dresses before they were completed, and returned the machine to Auntie Molly, who needed it in a hurry to do a job for a neighbour who was going on a holiday to Spain. She promised to finish the frocks for us as soon as she could, but she never seemed to get around to it, and in the end it was too late.

In order to make use of his time, Father began to work at home. He was building an extension to the kitchen. There was a heap of sand in one corner of the yard, and ten bags of cement, squat and of a particularly disgusting shade of grey, in another. The grass was covered with concrete blocks, which he made himself in a wooden mould and then left to dry in the sun. They emitted a sour, foul smell, a smell of winter, which wafted over to me as I played in the sand. I was building, too: palaces, villas in Spain, airports. I scraped out the runways with my hands, I fashioned little boundary walls, I built big terminals with flat roofs. I knew what an airport looked like, because we had got a television just before the strike had started. There was a home channel, we watched it every night from seven until it was time for bed. 'Joe Friday', 'The Donna Reed Show', 'The Honeymooners'. My airport was modelled on the one in Los Angeles.

Sometimes, of course, I played on the street, and I was there one day late in August, digging up melted tar with a lollipop stick, when Uncle Mick suddenly appeared at the corner. He came striding down the road, wearing his white trousers and blue blazer, as always in the summer. When he came close enough I could see that his eyes were twinkling just as usual, as if he were about to relate a very amusing joke.

'Where's Diana?' I asked immediately, forgetting my usual shyness, put on as a natural display of courtesy for all grown-ups.

'On me own this time, ducky!' he said. Then he picked me up and gave me a swing, and picked up Angela, who was smaller than me and who happened to be with me at the time, and gave her a leg and a duck. When we were both safely restored to the footpath, he handed me four shillings, one for each of us girls.

He winked.

'You pair run off and find Clare and Maura, get yourselves some sweeties! Mum and Dad in?'

I nodded. He walked down towards the house, and we ran to the shop on the next street to buy sweets.

For a shilling then you could purchase the following in the line of sweets: one small box containing ten filled milk chocolate sweets; two large bars of chocolate; three walnut whirls; four packets of crisps; six ice-pops; twelve penny-toffees; one hundred and twenty small sweets or bubble gums. Concentrating on the lower end of the market, we spent our shillings on lucky lumps, new potatoes, pineapple chunks, patsy pops. Then we sat on the kerb and ate the lot, not unhindered by our playmates, who were not above begging. They did it in vain. We'd had no sweets at all in several weeks. We felt entitled to a feast.

It was more than an hour later when Angela and I

arrived home: I had met our other sisters and given them their money, but they, being older, had departed for other more exotic shops in which to spend it. Uncle Mick had already left the house.

'Where is he?' I asked, disappointed.

'Gone back to where he came from, I hope,' my mother snapped. She was standing at the stove, stirring a saucepan of tomato soup. Her face was drawn and her hair greasy and plastered to her skull. It was a hot day. All days were hot, that summer.

'Why?' I asked, genuinely curious.

'None of your old backchat!' she retorted, somewhat unfairly. But in my mother's terminology in those days almost any unrequested comment counted as 'backchat', while silence was usually interpreted as 'cheek'. She turned towards me. 'What did he give you?'

'A shilling.'

'To all of yez?'

I sensed danger too late.

'Yes.'

'Where is the money?'

'Well . . .'

By now I was whining. Angela was on her way out the door.

'Where is it?'

'We spent it.'

'The whole shilling?'

She stared in disbelief. Her face was perfectly white. 'You spent a whole shilling on ould rubbish?'

I was running after Angela, out the door into the back garden. Mother gave chase, screaming at us. In the garden she grabbed a very long stick, which Father was using on his building project. She began to strike out at us with it. Father was pouring a bucket of water into a heap of cement. We ran to him, shouting: 'Save us! save us!', a formula we had been taught to use as babies. But he just looked at us distantly, hostilely, and said: 'You're very bold.' He did not understand the circumstances but he never took a stand against Mother. What he wanted from life was peace.

We ran out onto the street. Clare and Maura were there. Lots of children were there. They gazed at us, some with shock, most with a certain amount of apparent enjoyment. The boredom of an August afternoon, relieved in such a novel way! We ran down the middle of the road, crying. Mother pursued us, the long thin stick swaying above her like the mast of a storm-racked ship. She was no longer screaming, but sobbing violently. Like a child. Like us!

When we were almost at the corner, Father came out. He gently removed the stick from Mother's hand: it was part of a window-frame, he was probably afraid that it would break. He took her arm and led her back to the house.

Much later we all returned. Mother was in bed. It was tea-time, but we had no tea, because Father could not make any and neither could any of us. So we had bread and strawberry jam, which we ate in silence, sitting on the floor in the dining-room, watching 'Twilight Zone'. Then we too went to bed.

Shortly after that my mother got a job. 'Got a job' is the wrong phrase. She had married when she was eighteen, she had never had a paid job and lacked all qualifications. But she started her own business, making biscuits and selling them in the corner shop. She had always been a good cook. The biscuits sold well, and the business prospered, in a modest way. She got labels, she got boxes. The extension Father had built became a small home factory. She got a girl to help with the packaging and sales.

She did not, of course, get rich. But, instead of being drowned in the wave of prosperity that swept Ireland then, we rode along on top of it, with the other lucky ones. Life would have changed anyway. The strike ended, naturally. Father went back to work and earned a reasonable wage for the first time in his life. There was a loosening and expansion everywhere: swimming-pools appeared in the suburbs of Dublin, and we learned to crawl and do the breast-stroke. Education became free. I didn't have to slog and win a scholarship to go to secondary school or university. Anyone who was not stupid could go for nothing. I got a school uniform, I got a bicycle, I got clothes. In the end, I had a degree from Trinity, and a job in a school on the north side, and a boyfriend, from Surrey. Named Ross.

I went on a holiday with him and spent two weeks with his parents in the family home. It was two hundred years old, a house with timbered walls, covered in rosebuds of an old-fashioned, rare variety and blushing pink colour. Inside the cottage . . . they called it a cottage, although it had stairs, and ten rooms . . . were polished pine floors, handwoven rugs, thick oily landscapes in gilt frames. Ross's mother was a teacher in a grammar school, like me, more or less. His father was a management consultant, a profession the existence of which had been unknown to me before I'd met him.

We had a good holiday, as good as it could have been, under the circumstances. I fitted in as well as I fitted in anywhere. Indeed, the aloof manner I had developed over the years, the inevitable corollary of social climbing, seemed more natural here than it did in Dublin. Ross was aloof, too, and his parents even more so. Although surely for more admirable, less artificial, reasons than mine.

On the way home, we went to Yorkshire. I wanted to look at the Minster, I told Ross. And I wanted to see Diana and Auntie Jane. They were still living at Kingston Ridge, in Leeds. They had stayed there after the divorce, and Uncle Mick had moved to a flat in Bradford. I had seen none of them in years.

Kingston Ridge was what I had come to expect it to be: a neat row of council houses, much smaller than the houses in Exeter Place and with none of their fine Edwardian grandeur. But clean, cheerful, and, inside, furnished in comfortable bad taste. Bad? I mean different. Different from Ross's, and his parents. Different, now, from mine.

Auntie Jane brought us into her sitting room . . .

'lounge' . . . and we sat on the gold plush sofa and drank whiskey, while she perched on the edge of a chair, smoking. Her hair had become quite white, but her skin was still sallow, and she was thinner than ever.

'Long time no see, ducky!' she said.

I nodded vehemently into my whiskey. I was having difficulty in finding something to say.

'My word, you're looking well! Cut off all your nice hair, though, but I must say it suits you, it really does, dear.'

I should point out that at this stage I was as thin as Auntie Jane. I had learned how to diet, and had lost three stones during my last year at school. I was as elegant as I wanted to be. The problem was, when I lost weight my hair grew thin, too. It lost its richness and its lustre. Even its colour dimmed, so that instead of being a red-head, I was now, frankly, mousy. Auntie Jane was too tactful to comment on that.

'And how is Diana?' I asked, wondering, 'where is Diana?'

'Oh, she's fine, just fine, Diana is. In Spain on her holidays, she is, with her girlfriend, Pam. Just had a card from her yesterday: she's having a ball. Always does have, our Diana . . . She always has a good time.'

There was a photograph of her on the mantelpiece, several photos, in fact, one or two of which I recognised, since we had copies of them on our mantelpiece at home. A smiling face, small and plump, like Uncle Mick's. Carefree, like Uncle Mick's. And with a great mane of brilliant red hair framing it and falling over the sloping shoulders, pouring into the rim of the photograph, extending into infinity. Diana had not tampered with nature, and had been duly rewarded.

'What does she do now? Where does she work?'

Why did I have to ask that question?

'Why, she works with me, right here in Leeds. She works down at Northern Telephones, with me. She's in the office, of course. Typing.'

'That's nice.'

I drank. I was at sea. I couldn't find anything to say to Auntie Jane. For Ross's parents, for my colleagues, I had a line of smalltalk, I could always make some sort of conversation, however impoverished. But for Auntie Jane I had nothing. Ross was no help either. He sat back on the sofa and snorted into his drink, or rather drinks, because he took three in the course of ten minutes, the length of our visit. The shortest possible visit.

In the hall she whispered to me, 'Is this it, ducky?' nodding at Ross.

'Oh, I don't know,' I said, embarrassed. But I did know. I had known it already, probably, as I sat in the rose garden in Surrey, drinking herbal tea and chatting aimlessly about different kinds of roses with Ross and his reserved, precious parents. And in Auntie Jane's sitting room my suspicion was confirmed, as I struggled for words and Ross did not, but drank three glasses of whiskey and did not say a word. I knew all right. I knew too well, and much too much. And there was no one to whom I could talk, whose language I actually knew. I'd never had much for Auntie Jane. As a child I had been trained not to speak to adults at all, and, anyway, she had been separated from me, by space and age, and by money. Her money. And now I was separated from her by my money and by other, new, barriers. From her, from my parents, from Angela and Maura and Clare. And from Ross as well.

I am familiar with the present unemployment statistics. I know the amount of dole a family of four receives. And I live near a Corporation estate, I see the children running around the shopping centre. I see the mothers, in their jeans and jumpers, pushing around their buggies. Picking up burgers and frozen chips. I know they're poor, very poor, probably much poorer than I ever was. But I believe it's different now, poverty. I have to believe that. I think it's less baneful, less miserable. I don't think poor people feel guilty about it themselves, they're not ashamed of themselves. And they know there are alternatives.

I see the children running in and out of the sweet-shops, clutching tenpenny bags. I must presume that it's different.

A Visit to Newgrange

MUTTI WROTE to Erich. She would like to visit him in May. It had been two years since his last holiday in Bad Schwarzstadt and she was missing him. Besides, she was longing to see Ireland. A poster in the village travel agency depicted a scene in Connemara: a lake and hills and a donkey. The hills were so very green, she could hardly wait to climb them. And the sky was so very blue. And the donkey, so very friendly. It confirmed for her what she had always known, in her heart, about Ireland. She would arrive at 1.23 p.m. on the fourteenth, Flight E4327. Perhaps Erich could spare a few hours from his studies to come and meet her? She realised that he was very busy and if he couldn't manage it, why, she wouldn't mind. She was used to travelling alone now, ever since Vatti died (fifteen years previously). It was true that she was sixty-eight and suffered from severe arthritis of the hip. But she could get along very well on her own. Her English, at least, was rather good. That much she had to admit. She'd been taking lessons all winter, at the Bad Schwarzstadt Adult Education Centre. Of course, she'd never been to an English-speaking country before. Not since before the War, anyway, when she had stayed with a family in Devon, improving her command of the language. The father had been a doctor. He had died on D-Day, tending the wounded on a French beach.

She had written a long letter, apparently. I didn't see it myself. Erich relayed its contents to me, in a light, satirical tone he sometimes uses for comic effect. Probably he embroidered the details as he went along: he has a wonderful imagination.

Underneath his soft chuckles, however, lay a core of hysteria so blatant that I knew I was meant to take heed of it. Fear, I supposed it must be. Of Mutti. She was a little domineering, he had mentioned, once or twice? Oh, yes, indeed. With knobs on (Erich, like many speakers of English as a foreign language, possesses a rich store of colloquial expressions, and cannot resist employing them whenever possible). She was a real old battle-axe. Hard as nails. More demanding than a two-year old Ayatollah. More conservative than Maggie Thatcher. A dyed-in-the-wool Lutheran. More puritanical than John Knox.

I would have to move out.

It was only temporary.

She didn't realise he was living with me and the shock would be too much for her. Her only son. It was only for two weeks. Why make an issue of it? For a mere fortnight.

What about my mother? I politely enquired. She was dyed-in-the-wool Catholic, more conservative than John Paul the Second, more puritanical than Archbishop McNamara. She'd had to turn a blind eye on the fact that her daughter, her favourite daughter, her fifth daughter, was living in a state of mortal sin. She'd had to accept that life was different in Germany, different in Ranelagh, and soon would be different in Tuam, County Galway. And what about me, for heaven's sake? I was a dyed-in-the-wool Catholic, too, when you came to think about it, very deeply. Not just dyed, blued. Blued in the delicate, gauzy wool of the Virgin Mary's cloak: her blue-white, whiter-than-ordinary-white, artistically-draped, archetypal emblem of purity. A Child of Mary, that's what I actually was, called to her service in the chapel of Loreto on the Green when already a nubile impressionable fifteen-year-old. What about that? And what about integrity, courage and honesty, qualities which Erich claimed to prize above all others?

Mutti was sixty-eight. She had severe arthritis of the hip. It was only for two weeks. For heaven's sake.

On the thirteenth of May, I moved in with Jacinta who lives around the corner. On the fifteenth, Erich invited me up for a cup of tea, and I was introduced to Mutti.

She moved swiftly towards me, hobbling a little on the hip, and encircled me in a warm embrace. I don't hug people's mothers, or touch them at all if I can avoid it, and I was put off guard. Oblivious of my confusion, she smiled radiantly, and effused:

'It is so nice to see you! Erich tells me all about you this morning. Such a nice surprise for me! I did not know Erich has a girlfriend, you see. In Ireland, that is!'

I shook her hand gently: slight, bony and hot, two rocky protrusions on its third finger bit into my palm. I held on for a second, and examined Mutti. She was about five feet tall and fragile, with bountiful curly grey hair, large gentian eyes, innumerable glittering teeth. A bygone beauty. 'Bygone' in my estimation, that is, although probably not in her own, if my experience of her type is anything to go on.

'Now, we have a nice cup of tea!'

She had motioned me towards the sofa, a handsome tweed one which I had bought the winter before in Kilkenny Design. We sat down, and Erich put on the kettle. Just a cup of tea. They'd had dinner in town, he explained. Yes, yes, acquiesced Mutti, such an excellent meal. I had not had dinner in town. I'd had nothing since lunch, and then I'd had two crispbreads and a slice of cheese.

I glared at Erich behind her back and he lilted: 'Perhaps you'd like a sandwich? Are you hungry?' 'Oh not at all,' I replied icily. 'Don't go to any trouble on my account.' My bitterness was wasted on him: he has weather-proof sensibilities, and can, at the flick of some interior zip, protect himself from all atmospheric variation. (This ability is one of the qualities which encouraged me to love him). Blithely, he placed three mugs of tea, weak and tasteless, on the coffee table. We sipped it slowly, he and I marshalled up on the sofa opposite Mutti, who began her manoeuvres in oral English by requesting that I call her Friederika (I'd die first). Then she gave a full report of her trip from Germany and of the sightseeing tour she had taken that day. Questions of greater significance followed: were my parents still alive? What did my father do for a living? What was my own occupation? Rank? Salary? Quick but efficient. The cross-examination over, we ceded to her command that we watch television, since this would aid her in her battle with the language. Before I left, it was arranged that I should collect both Mutti and Erich the following morning and drive them to Newgrange, which Erich considered an essential ingredient of any Irish tour worth its salt, as he put it himself. Mutti had clapped her hands at the suggestion.

'Oh, yes. That would be so nice! Newgrange. I think Herr Müller mentions it. Is it near Spiddal?'

A month prior to her visit, Mutti had borrowed a guide-book from the public library in Bad Schwarzstadt. The work of one Heinrich Müller, it was entitled *Ein kleines irisches Reisebuch,* and she had studied it with single-minded diligence until she knew its contents by heart. It was to be her inseparable vade-mecum during her holiday, and her main criterion for enjoyment in sightseeing was that the sight had been referred to by Herr Müller.

Therefore she had merrily and gratefully limped through the litter of O'Connell Street ('oh! the widest street in Ireland!'), but the Powerscourt Centre had failed to arouse the mildest commendation. The Book of Kells had won her freshest laurels, but to the 'Treasures of Ireland' Exhibition, her reaction was one of chilled disappointment. 'Please, what is the meaning of the word "treasure?"' she had asked Erich, coming out of the museum onto Kildare Street. 'We did not have it in class, I believe.'

Herr Müller had spent the greater part of his *Reise* in Spiddal, and had devoted more than half his book, ten whole pages, to a graphic account of that settlement and its environs. Few corners of the western village were unfamiliar to Mutti, and she anticipated her sojourn there loudly and often and with the greatest of pleasure. Unfortunately, it would occur at the end of her stay in Dublin and last for no more than two days.

I arrived at the flat on the following morning, having taken a day's leave from my job in the Department of Finance.

'We'll go through the Phoenix Park,' I recommended brightly, determined to get value for my time. 'It's much more interesting that way, and only a bit longer. The President lives there. It's the biggest park in Europe.'

'Ah, yes,' responded Mutti noncommittally, as she settled into the passenger seat and opened a map. 'Can you show me where it is?'

I tried to lean across the brake and locate it for her, but Erich beat me to it, and, from the rear, indicated the relevant green patch. Mutti took a pencil from her handbag, held it poised in mid-air, and smiled: 'Are we going now?' On, James.

I drove to Charlemont Bridge.

'That's the canal,' I exclaimed brilliantly, waving at it as we turned off Ranelagh Road.

'Canal?'

'You know, Mutti. Canal. Not a river. Made by man. *Ein Kanal.*' Erich proferred the translation with caution: Mutti had decreed that no German be spoken in her presence, since this might sabotage her chances of commanding the language.

'It's called the Grand Canal,' I continued, pedantically.

'There are two canals in Dublin, the Royal and the Grand. This is the Grand. It's quite a famous canal, actually. Poems have been written about it. Good poems. Quite well-known poems.'

Alas, it was not the leafy-with-love part of canal, it was the grotesque-with-graffiti bit, and Mutti stared, bemused, at peeling mildewed walls and disintegrating furry corpses. Even if it had been picturesque, I don't think its high-falutin associations would have pulled any weight: Kavanagh had the misfortune to be post-Müller.

We drove towards Kilmainham in silence. The looming jail flooded my spirits with enthusiasm. The Struggle for Freedom was a favourite theme of Heinrich's, and Mutti, I had gathered from a few comments she had made, had also fallen victim to the romantic nostalgia for things Irish, historical, and bloody.

'Look!' I cried, 'there's Kilmain . . .'

But she had glimpsed the portico of the boys' school, which is impressive. And fake.

'Oh, Erich! How nice! Is it medieval, do you think?'

'Oh, yes, I think so, Mutti,' replied Erich, in his most learned voice. He knows nothing about Dublin, or architecture, or the Middle Ages.

'It looks like some of our German castles.'

'Look,' I pressed, 'that's Kilmainham Jail. The 1916 leaders were imprisoned there.' The light turned green. 'And shot,' I added, optimistically.

'In Bad Schwarzstadt we have two castles dating from the thirteenth century, Eileen, Marienschloss and Karlsschloss. They are so nice. People come to look from everywhere.'

'Really? I'd love to see them some day!'

The hint was ignored. I turned into the Park by the Islandbridge gate.

'This is the Phoenix Park,' the guided tour continued.

'Oh! A park. And we may drive in it. How nice.' Her tone was deeply disapproving. 'In Germany, we have many car-free zones. You know. Green zones, they are called. It is good without cars sometimes. For the health.'

At that moment, a Volkswagen sped around one of the vicious bends which are so common on the charming backroads of the Park. It took me unawares, and I was forced to swerve in order to avoid it. Swerve very slightly, and the Volkswagen was at fault.

'Oh, oh, oh, oh!' screamed Mutti, clapping her hands across her face. Through bony fingers her gentian eyes glared vindictively at me. I gritted my teeth and counted to fifty. Then I repeated fifty times 'a man's mouth often broke his nose', a proverb I had come across in *The Connaught Leader* a few weeks previously. Meanwhile, Mutti ignored the Pope's Cross, the clever woods, the flocks of deer gambolling in the clever woods, the American Embassy, the troops of travellers' ponies bouncing off the bonnet, the polo grounds and Áras an Uachtaráin.

'What town will we come to next?'

'Castleknock,' between one 'a man's mouth' and the next.

Scratch, scratch, went the pen on the map. Scratch scratch, through Blanchardstown, Mulhuddart, Dunshaughlin, Trim, past a countryside resplendent with frilly hedgerows, full-cream buttercups, fairy queen hawthorn, and, flouncing about everywhere, iridescent, giggling, fresh-from-Paris foliage. The sort of surrounding which sent many a medieval Irish monk into reams of ecstatic alliteration, as I liked to point out to my friends at this time of year, delicately reminding them that, even though I was a faceless civil servant, I had, in my day, sipped at the fountain of the best and most Celtic bards (taking a BA in Old Irish). Today I could practically smell the watercress and hazel. I could have taped the blackbird's song on my cassette. But I did not bother to emphasise the true Gaelic nature of the scenery for Mutti; tactfully leaving her to her own pedantic pursuits. Scritch scratch.

In County Meath we stopped for lunch. 'Ah,' gasped Mutti appreciatively, outside the 'olde worlde' hotel, 'this looks nice!' She guessed that an establishment with such a picturesque facade would have a high standard of cuisine. Alas, when we passed the promising threshold our eyes were greeted by a sign stating: 'lunch served in the bar', and our nostrils assailed by the ripe seedy odours of grease and alcohol. In Mutti's refined Lutheran opinion, drink was unspeakably Non-U, and her perfect nose wrinkled in disgust.

'Would you like something to drink, Mutti,' Erich asked, ordering two pints of Harp with great alacrity.

'Harp? What is that? Lemonade? Juice?'

'Well, no, it's a kind of light beer.'

'Juice. I will have some Harp juice, please. I am very thirsty.'

When the three drinks arrived, gleaming yellow and foaming over the edges, Mutti first clamped her lips together, then began to sip energetically. Service of the meal was slow, and she tapped her foot impatiently on the carpet.

'It is lucky I am not hungry. They are killing that pig for me, I think.'

In twenty minutes, the waitress arrived, bearing a dinner plate for Mutti, covered with slivers of pork and side dishes of carrots and cauliflower and cabbage and potatoes and gravy. She accepted generous helpings of everything . . . 'I am not hungry but I pay' . . . and, having dispensed with most of it, slid the leavings into a plastic bag which appeared, as if by magic, from her coat pocket: 'After all, we pay,' she said, not bothering to whisper. 'I eat this for lunch tomorrow. A little meat, that is all I need, now that I am older. I have a small appetite.'

Erich and I finished our salads hastily, and we proceeded to Newgrange.

It does not disappoint. Me. There are many among my

acquaintance who hate it. They prefer Knowth and Dowth. Goethe. Shabby Victoriana. Woodworm. I relish the lambent, urbane face of immortality: Newgrange, pretentious crystal palace, lording it over the fat cowlands, the meandering fishbeds, reflecting the glory of the sun without a shadow of suburban modesty.

Erich, although he pays lip-service to its archaeological significance, belongs to the group of those who feel uneasy with this example of prehistoric P.R.; he senses that it is in dubious taste. I would not have been surprised to find Mutti of like mind. But no:

'It is very nice,' she gasped, to Erich, as we climbed the hill to the tumulus.

'I knew you'd like it, Mutti,' he simpered, his eyes rivetted to the figure of the guide, a slender and provocative one, neatly glazed in luminous yellow pants and white T-shirt. She posed on a standing stone outside the mound and outlined its history in a few well-chosen words, then led the creeping party of tourists along the narrow passage to the burial chamber. Mutti had been pleased by the outside of the grave, but she was in raptures within. The ice-cold room at the centre of the hill enchanted her soul, and she oohed and ahed so convincingly that the lemon-clad one directed her remarks expressly at her, catching her large eyes and ignoring the other, less charming, members of the little group. When her spiel was over and she made the mandatory request for questions, only one was asked, and that by Mutti:

'Are there any runic stones here?' How silly, I thought. But, of course, there were. It was possible that one stone at the side of the vault contained writing. Had the guide invented this titbit to satisfy Mutti? Hardly. She had an honest, if tarty, face.

After the tour, Mutti and I lingered in the burial chamber. The others left, gradually, but she seemed to want to stay, and I felt it my duty to remain, too. What with her arthritis. Gradually, however, I realised that I was happy to be in the cool greyness of the place. It has, I noticed for the first time, a curious intimacy, the character of a kitchen, a space at the centre of the home where people gather to sustain themselves. To survive. And, although it is as chill as a tomb . . . it is a tomb, after all . . . this room has a hearth, a focus: the guide had explained that once a year the sun would pour through the opening in the outer wall, stream along the entrance passage, and flood the chamber with light. Illumination for the immortal dead.

Mutti, tracing with her delicate fingers the spiralling patterns on the tombstones, turned to me:

'Imagine how nice it is here on December twenty-one. So very nice!'

Her eyes glowed with a candour they had not held before, and for the first time since our meeting we looked at each other full in the face. We laughed. Mutti moved towards me slowly, because of the hip, and I had an impulse to run and embrace her, to kiss her. She would not have been embarrassed, that was the sort of thing she did. But I do not kiss people's mothers, or touch anyone at all, if I can avoid it. So I hesitated.

Erich crept into the chamber. Mutti hobbled over to him and clasped his hand.

'It's time to go,' he said. 'Haven't you had enough of this creepy old mausoleum?'

So brief are our moments of salvation. So sudden. So easily lost.

A Fairer House

I LIVE IN A forge, a blacksmith's forge. I'll describe it for you as precisely as possible: you have a taste for the detailed, the accurate, the scientific.

It is built of large granite stones. They were quarried locally, from time to time as the need arose, and all the walls were made to last forever. The stones are white-washed. Streaks of grey show through the wash in patches where the wind and rain have beaten hard. Except on the southern, sheltered side of the house, the part I now inhabit. Green moss covers it, and no stone is visible.

Architecturally, the place is built in what is known in the literary home counties as the folly style. You know, old chap, King George's Folly and Queen Anne's Folly and Stella Gibbons's Folly and all that? 'Folly', in any of its senses, is not a very popular word in the Northern Irish idiom, but it most aptly describes my forge: it is built without pattern or purpose. Generations of my ancestors have fashioned it thus. Good blacksmiths and hapless architects, all of them. There are twenty odd misplaced rooms in the house. Too many, you think? I would thrive in a house with a hundred thousand rooms, if they were constructed with the efficiency of cells in a beehive. But in this house, there *are* too many. Predictably, the single well-situated room is the forge itself. It is placed right in the centre of the roundabout. It used to be a crossroads, but habits change. Now it is a roundabout. With a stream channelled to encircle it. You would have guessed, I suppose. You would know that I must live on the roundabout, although you have never come here. You would know it stands to reason.

The forge is dead. It hasn't been used in donkey's years. There are a few horses and asses on the hill farms hereabouts: some tourists pony-trek in summer. But the animals are not shod at my forge. It could be done. The anvil is still there, and an enormous hammer, and tongs for the fire. They are made of heavy, rusty iron. Nobody would dream of taking them, although the main door is always open and people come and go. A few horseshoes are lying around on the floor. Children who are brought by their parents to look at the place and improve their minds have a habit of picking up the horseshoes and letting them drop with a clang on the flags. The clangs resound eerily through every corner of the house. Their echoes penetrate to the marrow of my bones and fill me with death-shivers even in the middle of summer. Fortunately, people do tend to take the filthy things away with them. They hang them over the halldoor or the fireplace, for good luck. I can't believe in the superstition, but I'm glad others do. The sooner the horseshoes all disappear, the better. I hate them.

There is nothing else in the forge, not one cobweb. It has remained peculiarly clean and shining over the years. It may owe this to the constant traffic of tourists, day in, day out. Overawed by the coldness and darkness of the place, which has an atmosphere akin to that of a passage-grave, they don't litter the place with their sweet-wrappers and potato-crisp bags. But their feet polish the flags and their collected breath sweeps off the dust and cobwebs. Maybe that is it.

Sometimes, however, in odd moments between waking and sleeping, I wonder. I suspect that the ghosts of my ancestors sneak back when the smithy is empty, and do a quick spring-clean job with God-knows what brooms and feathers from beyond the grave. Whatever it is, it's not me: I never lift a finger to clean the place. I find hygiene harmful to the spirit.

Around the forge, rooms are strung haphazardly; some are one, some two, some three or four storeys high. One room at the top of a third storey is inaccessible except by ladder or wing. As far as I know, nobody has ever slept there and the reason for its existence escapes me entirely. A lunatic whim. There are crows nesting in the room, in the large bed. It surprises you, that crows should live indoors, rather than on the tops of trees? In this part of the country, on the hilly northern coast, tall trees are few and far between. Crows would be glad of a comfortable double-bed.

The other rooms are all accessible by the human foot, either from within or without the building. They are of varying shapes and sizes, but mainly small. You couldn't swing your cat — fluffy white Mollser — in any of them. How can I describe the rooms? A bedroom in the north wing is furnished simply, like an Irish country room, with timbered floor and walls and a sugán chair and a wooden bedstead. A drawingroom in the west has Persian rugs, velvet drapes, and a myriad crystal lamps. Every room is different and quite individual. Forget them, you will learn all you need to know as I ramble on. The single important point to remember is the maze of corridors and staircases. Horrifying. They wind this way and that, narrow and gloomy, frightening to traverse. Some lead to every room in the house (except to the crow's nest); some lead nowhere at all, but bring you after hours of breathless wandering to a solid thick wall, or worse still, to a narrow window opening onto the sharp air twenty feet up. That is what you must really bear in mind: corridors.

I have been living in a room in the south-west corner

of the house for three years now. Exactly three years, in fact, because today is the 25th of May. Before that, I used to change my abode more frequently, partly because I enjoyed change, partly to keep as much of the house as I could bear to live in aired. Now I find only the warm southern light congenial, and the room, soft as a silk-worm's cocoon, is my home. I eat and sleep there, and keep my specimens in a small ante-room. The little pond animals thrive in the sweet warm atmosphere. Science flourishes in contentment. You, practical, realistic, could understand that. You know what life requires.

Three years ago I lived in the north wing, in an attic studio. The back wall was shelved, and filled with books. The outside wall was made of glass. In the clear northern light, I could paint all day if I wanted to. And I was into painting then, in a big way. Landscapes and seascapes. I used to go off to the mountains or down to the shore with my sketching pad and camera (there's a darkroom here) and from sketches and photographs I made watercolours. The works were a commercial success. I sold a good many of them at a gallery in Dublin, and was beginning to attract a small circle of admirers. Occasionally, I had a bash at portraits; I'd go down to the roundabout and sketch the passing drivers. But they had a sameness about them, and the smell of exhaust fumes, and the aura of stewed tea and packed lunches nauseated me. I concentrated on scaping.

The 25th of May three years ago was an exceptionally fine day. Strong sun, blue sky, light breeze, cotton-wool clouds: the scene has been set often enough before. If your memory fails you ask your local librarian for a reference. Conditions being thus favourable, I took to the hills. Dressed in my artist's apron, with all my gear under oxter, I crossed the roundabout, the bedraggled farms, the pock-marked bogs. I climbed the spongy slopes that led to the hilltop. There, in a glen high up between two ranges, is a beautiful lake.

It is black and deep, and nothing grows in it except for a few reeds on one side. I have since discovered that it contains excellent examples of a rare type of snail, but to the layman's eye it is as pure and barren as ice. The sudden clouds and the shadows which darted uneasily across the hills were always reflected in its surface, itself smooth at one moment and rippling madly at the next: a totally unpredictable phenomenon, my one compensation for the brutally changeable weather conditions in this part of Ireland. On the day in question, the lake moved me to lyricism. My mind teemed with Wordsworthian jargon: words like 'mighty,' 'tranquillising,' 'empyrean', and the like. The fact is that the beauty of it bit right into my senses, hard, making my eyes swim and my heart chuckle wildly. Joy, you'd call it.

I washed my hands in the lake to wake me out of the semi-stupor of the feeling. The water was ice cold. It startled me to action and I worked vigorously all day. Sketched and snapped from every height and angle. In the evening, with five full reels and a bulging pad, I strode home to the forge. A satisfied man. Not even the family cars, hurtling noisily around the roundabout, could shift my sense of fulfilment.

As I approached the house, I was thinking of my dinner. Smoked salmon, oaten bread, dry white wine. A meal to celebrate the height of summer. And to satisfy my ravenous hunger.

I entered the house through a small ivy-screened door at the back. I was reluctant to use the main door; I never knew what fourth cousin might be lurking in the forge, waiting to be invited up for tea and cakes. Himself and a family of six, perhaps. All busily dropping horseshoes on the floor.

In fact the house was quiet. It was clear that nobody had come to spoil my happy day. As I walked up the longest corridor winding up four storeys to the studio, I hummed a bit of a tune. Beethoven's *Andante molto moto,* the cuckoo-ish bit. Which should indicate the direction of my joy-curve to you. You know how rarely I sing.

I opened the door of the studio, humming away. Suddenly I heard a sound. I stopped, voice, heart, all.

From the depths of the house, sweet high notes rose. My fright was intense. I wanted to leap through the glass wall of my studio to the ground below. To lie on the ground in fragments for the motorists to gaze at, maybe report to the nearest garda station, twenty miles away. I've mentioned the strange cleanliness of the forge. Did you know, the anvil is reputed to contain all the notes of the violin, if tapped in the right spots? By the right person. An ancestral spectre. You may laugh, but this house is an ancient, odd place, where I have often lost track of time and sense. For a minute I was witless.

The notes gradually crystallised and I realised they were produced by a human voice. A warm girl voice. Listening, the chilly fear melted. I tried to pinpoint the location of the voice. Impossible. It floated through the atmosphere of the house as if it emanated from the walls and floorboards and rafters. Suffusing me. Creeping through the orifices of the body, the pores of the skin, right into the bloodstream. Whirling faster and faster through me, exciting me utterly and compelling me to comb the house from top to bottom in search of the singer. I traversed every corridor. I ploughed through corridors full of cobwebs, spiders and insects. I slid along the glazed surfaces of highly polished corridors. I choked on the dust of stinking, carpeted corridors. I opened doors I hadn't opened in years and doors I had never opened in my life till then. I saw rooms of magnificent splendour and rooms of terrible dinginess and filthy little holes of sculleries and dungeons that filled me with dread. I battled with the hang-ups and fears of a lifetime, in the attempt to reach the voice.

Finally I found her. In the room where I now live. A shaft of light shone through the west window and bathed her. Not a ghost or a vision. A solid young woman of twenty. Straight fair hair. Suntan. Jeans and gingham. She was sprawled on a cushioned armchair, a guitar at her side. She stopped singing, when I walked in and looked at me, quite coolly, considering the circumstances, she being a trespasser and liable to prosecution for breaking and entering. Possibly with intent to burglary. How was I to know? My house is a repository of antique articles which would fetch good prices on any market. But of course burglars do not sing in high penetrating tones and play the guitar.

The ecstatic frenzy of the search had left me, and I felt ill at ease and nervous. Not knowing what to say, I took refuge in banalities and mumbled a 'good evening' with as much sang-froid as I could muster.

I asked her who she was.

'Emily. My name is Emily.' An American accent.

'And, what are you doing in this part of the world?' Not to be too blunt about it.

'Touring. I've been touring the Irish coastline for a week.'

'Mm.'

'I came to the roundabout there this afternoon. I saw the house, and decided to come and take a look. It looks so interesting.'

Relief flooded me. The totally ordinary.

'People often do,' I said. 'It used to be a forge. You've probably seen that already.'

'Yeah. I noticed it on the way in. Then I started to explore the corridors.'

And got lost, I supposed. The conversation continued at this level for ten minutes, until my hunger suddenly nipped me like a monstrous crab. I asked her to join me in the north studio.

'I'd love to eat. I'm starving. But I'd rather not go to the north studio.'

'You haven't even seen the north studio . . . have you?'

She smiled that little shy smile always used by a woman who has dug her heels in and knows she will get her way, however unreasonable it is, in a matter of minutes. She gazed vacantly over the roundabout, still buzzing with cars, to the darkening hills.

'I like this room,' she said.

I left it at that, and carried the food, the crockery, and the stereo down from the north studio.

'Oh, fabulous,' she said when she spotted the salmon. Her vocabulary seemed limited to the five hundred words necessary for survival.

'I love smoked salmon with wine. Is it dry?'

'Very.' I winked . . . I never wink but she was that kind of girl . . . and poured it. Put a disc on the stereo. Beethoven's 'Pastoral'.

She jumped up and pirouetted about the room for a minute or two, nicely, as if she had had some ballet training.

We fell upon the food. She was as hungry as I was, and ate and drank with as much gusto. Half an hour later, we were full and slightly drunk. An hour later, we were in each other's arms. Two hours later, in bed.

I hadn't made a decision. Emily made all the initial moves, and I easily and gratefully followed. It surprises me, because I am not physically a very attractive man. But there is no other explanation for the fact of my being under the silk with her . . . the bed had silk sheets . . . on that night three years ago I would not have considered seducing her.

Afterwards, I wondered had the room been deliberately selected. Because, while other rooms in the house have beds, couches, easy-chairs, soft carpets, none but the south-west room had silken sheets. Or such delicate lamps, such warm, honey-rose light. A real love room. Could it have been only a chance that she found the most seductive chamber?

Making love to Emily was a marvellous experience. I cannot describe more accurately the bliss of the night. It was as if all the joys of the day — the warm light, the darting shadows, the 'Pastorale' . . . and all her flaxen hair and golden body, smooth girl body, absorbed me, so that I ceased to be and became . . . her. Ecstasy? More hot and human than ecstasy. I cannot describe it. Then afterwards, no little death. Just a deep long sleep, from which I awoke hours later, totally refreshed.

Emily was gone. This didn't surprise me. She had got up and gone to find a toilet or shower or something. If so, she was probably lost at this stage, sitting alone and frightened in some poky room or at the end of a cul-de-sac corridor. Maybe crying.

I got up lazily . . . I felt peaceful . . . and set off to look for her. Calling her name softly as I moved along the maze of corridors and the twisting staircases. I travelled farther and farther away from the south room, and still got no answer to my calls. Anxiety grew. For the second time in twenty-four hours I opened every door, trudged along every corridor, climbed every staircase. Always hoping that I would open a door and find her. Weeping, laughing, singing, dancing, sleeping: anything, only to find her.

I left the north studio until the end, partly because she had objected so strongly to it, partly because of a vague feeling that she might have gone there out of female curiosity. The last hope. I looked in. Sunlight shone strongly on my easels, portfolios, brushes. No Emily. I walked over to the glass wall and looked out. A car was parked down below. Funny. I hadn't noticed a car the night before. Emily's car? Was she still in the house? Or in the garden? Hiding?

Suddenly, as I mused, a note struck my ears. Hope plunged into my blood. Then a second note sounded. A high, clanging note. Ringing up through the house. Penetrating to the marrow of my bones. Hell! A horseshoe thrower. A bloody party of bloody mealy-mouthed little brats throwing horseshoes on the floor of my forge.

I cracked up then. In my dressing-gown and slippers I ran screaming from the forge and to the main road. Like a madman. Hailed the passing cars. None of them stopped. Not surprisingly, I suppose, but I stayed for hours and hours. Until finally you came along. In your red Ford. So calm, cool, understanding. You put me on the back seat and gave me a sedative. Said I'd just had a bit of a shock, everything would be O.K. Burglars, I said. A burglar called Emily. Did you know her? You said yes, yes, in soothing tones like treacle and brought me to the cosy cottage hospital to get over the shock. Introduced me to your cat. No questions asked, treatment administered gently and effectively until I became . . . O.K. Then you began to urge me to pull myself together and go home. Kind, level-headed, sympathetic. You persuaded me to come back.

I have lived in this south room ever since. In its glow there seemed to be a bit of peace. Around me the maze of corridors, the twenty empty rooms, the hum from the roundabout, the clangs from the forge. With me, the memory of her, and my samples. Pond-life, science: cool, comprehensible, helps me get a grip on things, keep everything hanging together.

But now I've got to tell you something quite important. I've never wanted to live in this house. That day on the roundabout, I wanted to make a getaway. I wanted to become a roundabout person and drive around in a family saloon and eat ham sandwiches for evermore. And you picked me up off the roundabout, and you persuaded me to return to the forge.

Tomorrow I will leave the south room. I will creep along the dark maze of corridors to a deep black chamber. I will creep deeper and deeper into the awful heart of my house. Until I am lost for good.

Unless . . . you come again, to take me away.

Roses are Red

WHEN I drive into town I listen to the radio. Sometimes to cassettes, but mostly to the radio. That's the only time I do listen to it, really. The reason, as you know, is that I live very far away from the city centre, and that the journey is long and bloody boring. Once I used to enjoy it, soon after I learned to drive, but I certainly don't any more. Frankly it drives me to distraction. Or it would, were it not for the radio. Let's hope it never cracks up!

Well! It was Valentine's Day so this fellow was going on and on about the language of flowers. A red rose means love, for instance. So what's new? Thirteen roses. They mean true devotion. And cost, of course, about thirty quid. Then there's the convolvulus. Oh, yes, that's what he said. A bit of ivy and a scrap of straw. They symbolise a united marriage. Of what? A couple of scare-crows?

These corny phony topical chats make me sick.

I switched stations. On Radio Two Vera Lynn was singing an 'I'm a demented Housewife' song. Had a pretty good chorus:

'One needs a cookie
And one needs a changing
And one is on the way!'
She ended with a fantastic shriek:
'My God, I hope it's not twins, like the last time!'

I liked it, I really did. And I wondered where I could get hold of a copy of the song. I considered writing to the radio and making an inquiry, but became realistic after one set of lights and gave up the idea. I never bother, in the end, about things like that. Too much trouble, and also I haven't got the energy. No doubt records by Vera Lynn can't be had for love or money nowadays. She's stacked away in some archive somewhere, I'll bet, going putrid, dragged out for Valentine's Day and other special occasions. Or am I wrong? Really I know next to nothing about the woman, it's just that her name suggests my mother's generation. And her song suggested that too, in a way. The odd thing is, though, the life Vera Lynn was screaming about was actually much more like mine than like my mother's. Which is the same as saying that I live in the style of an American housewife of half a century ago, or so. My mother certainly never enjoyed that way of life. I know, I was a kid then, I remember what it was like.

The atmosphere was simply, absolutely, totally different. You know what I mean? No, you don't, because in Sweden it was much closer to being American than to being Irish, I'll bet my bottom dollar. Well, what I mean is, we didn't have any cookies. Not what you'd have called cookies. Broken biscuits in white stiff bags from Jacobs, maybe; *Marietta* and *Kimberley*, from tins with glass tops in the grocer's shop . . . which had sawdust on the floor, by the way, and baskets full of straw with eggs nestling in them on the counter, and huge blocks of butter from which the grocer, a man in an overall the colour of sawdust, hacked a pound for you when you wanted it and then wrapped it in a bit of greaseproof paper. 'A little over a pound, Mam, will that do?' I don't know, of course, but I don't think your mother, in downtown Stockholm or wherever, was getting, 'a little over a kilo, Mam,' in those days. Or Vera Lynn. I just can't believe Vera Lynn was living like that then. She was getting a phone call from her husband, for heaven's sake . . . in the song, this was in the song . . . saying he was bringing a colleague home for dinner. Jesus! We didn't have a phone when I was a kid, hardly anybody did. And dinner was a meal we had at one o'clock in the day. My father came home to it, all right. Every single day, on the thirteen bus from the newspaper office in O'Connell Street where he worked. We didn't have colleagues home to dinner. Or home to anything. If we had guests at all, it was to tea on Sundays, for fairy cakes and tomato sandwiches. And they were always relations, or as good as. Friends did not visit, in that sense. And colleagues! We didn't even think anyone had colleagues.

But now we do. Jim has loads of them. And they do come to dinner, expectedly and unexpectedly, as you know only too well. And we do have dinner at night, just like Vera Lynn, and I do scream and shout and rant and rave about the kids, just like her. Oh, yes, my life is American, it sure is. It's just one bottomless 'Old-Fashioned', that's what it is.

So. I reached town at long last, and I found a parking place on the Green, without difficulty, it being a Saturday, and then I walked along under the trees for a bit and down Kildare Street towards the Library. And I want to tell you that at this point my mood changed completely. All my little irritations just vanished into thin air. You see, I really love town on Saturday mornings. I can't tell you how much I love it, it's one of those feelings that are very very intense in me and at the same time seem so silly that I just can't express them to anyone. I mean, what the hell's so wonderful about town on a Saturday? But it is wonderful, for me anyway. It's that fresh unspoiled look it has, like a kid after a bath, you know. Innocent. Earth has not anything to show more fair and so on. At eleven o'clock Kildare Street is still at that kind of dawn of the day, Wordsworthian stage, as long as it's the weekend. And so quiet. It just calms me down.

Of course, I had that guilty feeling I always get when I don't have a buggy to push, or Kelly dragging at the hem of my coat. My conscience tells me that I ought to be harrassed by kids all the time, that I should be dragged down to the earth by their little pulling paws. And I was so far from earth! I was, believe it or believe it not, right up there in heaven. Between those high buildings that block out the sun, reduce everything to a bureaucratic cypher, I feel saved. And once I'm in the library, I get the feeling that it's for eternity! Some delusion, but there you are. Not that it's a particularly delightful surrounding. I know more attractive bibliotheks. Yours, for instance. That always made me think of the first glorious pages of some medieval manuscript, an illuminated one, I mean. All those quaint flowers, gillyflowers and columbines and hollyhocks and such, in such quaint old-fashioned colours. Magenta. Ochre. Indigo. The inks of scribes. It's such a fantastic thing, to have a garden in front of a library. A full colour frontispiece! Then the mellow face of yellow brick. The vellum title page. Our institution reminds me of a volume of parliamentary papers, to tell you the truth. Or a collection of law tracts. Solid and authoritative, with its thick grey pillars and thick grey walls. No windows. No imagination.

But inside it's quite all right. It's more than all right, it's quite delightful. In fact, inside, it's very much like your place, really. The same gracious curves and wide spaces. The same pastel colours on the walls, and warm wooden furniture. Oh yes, and the atmosphere is very pleasant too. Especially when the place is not too busy. A sense of calm and order prevails, and I'm very partial to a sense of calm and order. After my less than tidy home lifestyle, it suits me very well indeed.

As I sat at my desk and waited for the books I'd ordered, I fancied myself a Victorian scholar, whose day was regulated by the comings and goings of the attendant in his navy blue coat, and by the big hands of the library clock. I gloried in it. Not that what I was doing was all that exciting. You certainly wouldn't call it scholarship. It was a bit of boring old genealogical research I had to do for an American cousin of mine. You know this awful roots craze? I was telling you about it once, you probably wouldn't remember. But maybe you come across it over there too. Anyway, I have dozens of cousins and relations of one kind and another in America and they're always looking for information about the past which we can't give them. I'd promised this fellow months before that I'd help him. He wanted some proof that he was descended from Brian Boru. Scottie O'Brien, his name is, did you ever in your life? He's a fourth cousin, thanks be to God. So I wrote out about six dockets and I was sitting down waiting for the books to arrive. I certainly didn't think much of my chances of success. But I was going to give it two hours. What I could spare. And then I was going to write to him and say it was no go. Everyone called O'Brien is a descendant of Brian Boru anyway. It's just not that easy to get proof, in individual cases . . . that's what the fellow on the issue desk had told me. He probably knew what he was talking about. These guys do.

I didn't see you entering the reading room. But I saw you shortly afterwards, I'd guess, standing at the desk, writing out dockets. I was looking up from my work then, bored after only about fifteen minutes, and I saw the back of your head bent over the desk.

I do like the back of your head.

Sometimes, when I'm driving along, I don't listen to the radio. I sing. I sing a song in Irish that contains this line:

'How lovely for the ground her shoe walks upon!'

But I change the possessive pronoun to the masculine form and I sing:

'How lovely for the gallery my love goes along

And how lovely for the ground his shoe walks upon!'

And there's also a very nice bit about the blossom of the sloe, which I'm attached to, I am not quite sure what sloe blossom looks like but you remind me of it anyway. Sloe blossom. Hawthorn blossom. All kinds of blossom. Why should these images be used only of women? You remind me of them. Sloe blossom. So I change the pronouns. At the beginning I used to slip up and sing them in the wrong gender occasionally but after a while I got it right. Now if anyone asked me . . . and of course they don't, I'm no singer . . . I'd say that was a feminine song. But it's really a masculine song. Or is it? Or is there such a difference? I'm only asking.

I wished you'd turn around . . . I wanted to get a proper look at your face. I've always had a problem with your face, you see, and as a matter of fact this is a problem I've had with any face I've loved. I can't remember it. Not as a fixed feature, an image which pops into my mind along with your name. No. I can, or I could, or I can . . . remember it on specific occasions. I think. That first time I saw you, for instance. That time Jim had rung up from the office and said he was bringing a colleague home for dinner. Oh yes, he does it all the time. Typical careerist. I was cross, as usual when we have visitors. I was quite in a heap by the time you arrived. Literally I was in the bedroom, delving into a pile of clothes on the floor, trying to get something to put on. My hair was wet and I was worried about whatever I had in the oven, and I could hear the voices in the hall, yours and Jim's. I had to hurry up, to grab something and put it on, and then to lay aside my sour mood and pretend to be convivial, to come down the stairs from my real self to the drawing room of my party personality.

I opened the door of the living-room. There was your face. Outlined against the blue curtains. I had not been expecting it, that's all I can say. What had I been expecting? Well, I don't know. But not that. White skin. Perfect features. Blond hair. And your eyes.

There are words for eyes like yours, you know. 'Come abed.' 'Charismatic'. All the great lovers, the Don Juans, have them. But those words do not quite describe your eyes, and using them doesn't incapacitate the reality at all, the way words sometimes do. They're so incredibly powerful. I've seen them in action since that time. I've watched women rivetted to your gaze, perfectly sensible women, blushing and burning. You do know this, don't you? You must. But the first time, I didn't. I took it that your ardour was for me.

And it was. At the time. It's just that there are a lot of women. The time is short.

Are you not weary of ardent ways?

You probably are. But they're not. And I was not.

I sat at my table and tried to concentrate. But when only an hour had elapsed I handed in my books and left the library. Without a backward glance. I hoped, of course, that you would see me. That your eyes were on my back. I hoped it so much that I felt them between my shoulder blades. As I walked down the staircase, which is an ideal staircase for a lover to walk down, wide and sweeping, I listened for the sound of your footsteps. I was expecting to feel, at any minute, the pressure of your hand on my shoulder.

But I didn't.

I walked down Molesworth Street, along Anne Street.

The path was bathed in pale lemony sunlight. The cold air nipped my nose, but carried to it a lovely smell, the smell of roasting coffee beans. The best smell in the world. Especially on Anne Street, on a Saturday. When you smell coffee roasting, your heart lifts. You know there is hope for the future. You know, above all, that foreign lands exist and that you will visit them all, someday.

Good isn't it? I've borrowed it from a book by some Icelandic author whose name escapes me. You don't happen to know who he is? Do you ever read Icelandic authors? Some Swedes do.

I stopped at a bookstall. I am, after all, very bookish. I don't say I'm an intellectual, I don't say I'm a scholar, God knows I'm neither of these things. But I am, in my humble way, literate. Coming from a library, I have to stop at every bookshop I pass, just to check it out. In case I'd miss anything. I have to browse.

This was a second hand shop, specialising in paperbacks of an unacceptably popular nature. Unacceptable to me, that is. I'm an awful snob about fiction. This is another of the forms my literacy takes. I read nothing but novels, easy novels in the English language, but they have to be real. Not Cartland, Krantz, not even Le Carré. If I wanted his sort of stuff, well, really, I'd much rather just reread Graham Greene, who did it before, and in an acceptably popular form. Acceptable to me, that is.

The books were stacked on trestle tables, spines to the sky, and I scanned the titles, idly. To my surprise there was a copy of *The Works of Thomas Mann*, back to back with Jeffrey Archer. A big fat vulgar paperback, containing about six different novels, all crammed in together in tiny illegible print. Still, it cost only eighty pence and included a novella called *The Black Swan* which I hadn't read. So I went into the shop and bought it. And then I stood there in the middle of the grotty little place and searched for a bit I like in *Death in Venice*. It's this:

'Beauty, and beauty alone, Phaedrus, is lovely and visible at once. It is all our senses can perceive on earth, or bear to perceive.'

I'm not quite sure that I know what that means. All our senses can perceive? Has Mann left out something? I'm not sure that I agree with it anyway. But I'd noted it before, the day after that day you came to dinner, actually, and it had seemed all right then. Not just all right. Quite right.

I closed the book and emerged onto the street. And that's when I bumped into you.

We confronted each other face to face.

We said hello.

You asked me if I'd like coffee.

I said yes.

No. That is not what happened. It's what I'd like you to think, what you have thought, perhaps. The truth was somewhat less serendipitous. My experience, after all, with life and with men is quite extensive, and it has taught me above all else that fate and fortune should not be relied upon in affairs of the heart. Management is required. I often think that it's girls who don't realise this simple fact in time that get left out in the cold, don't you agree? Or who do realise it but are too honest or refined or something to operate accordingly. I'm not. Honest. And the truth is, I tailed you from the Library. I saw you get up to leave, I followed you down the stairs and along Molesworth Street. When I saw you vanish into that sweetshop, on Anne Street, I popped into the book market next door and lay in wait. Thumbing through novels to pass the time. All that stuff about Thomas Mann is a fabrication. Shops like that don't sell Thomas Mann, they simply don't.

I thought you'd never come out of the sweetshop. You seemed to be in there for half an hour at the very least. But you did emerge, finally, and you did ask me for coffee, and I did, of course, since it's what I'd been angling for, say yes. With a surge of triumph. Triumph, and what often accompanies it: despair.

We went to that Italian place, where they serve spaghetti and chips and expresso. The main smell is of grease. There isn't a hint of herbs or garlic, or anything of that romantic nature. And there is absolutely no smell of coffee. Expresso doesn't seem to have a smell. I'm not surprised. It doesn't have a taste, either. Not the real strong Northern European taste I enjoy.

The place was crowded. We had to sit at a tiny table near the kitchen. Delph clattered, people chatted and seemed to scream at one another, the coffee machine hissed vindictively. I told you about the work I'd been doing and you told me about yours: looking up some old advertisement feature in a newspaper which related to the agency, wasn't it? And then you told me about a play you'd been to in the Abbey and how much you liked Irish drama. Then the coffee came in small cups, and you talked some more. But I couldn't hear what you were saying. It was so noisy. So hot and crowded and noisy.

I could, however, see your face. It had a kind of luminosity of its own, in that dark little dive. It shone, really, against the grimy walls, among the dark Irish faces, the dark Italian faces. Fair faces, fair hair, have some kind of lambent quality which other kinds of complexions don't have. I can understand why the blond is the ideal, everywhere it has ever existed. It's almost magical.

You were talking, about plays, I think, and your eyes were gleaming and your hands gesticulating. I saw you looking into your cup, judging, and I knew you were preparing to leave. After only five minutes! That's when I panicked. You put down the cup with a little final clink and I leaned across the table. The coffee machine hissed. The waiters shouted. I said it.

You looked at me and your eyes clouded. For a split second. Then you said: 'Sorry, I did not quite catch that!' The machine hissed. You are such a gentleman. You did not quite catch it.

'It was nothing,' I murmured, finishing my coffee. And we left the cafe.

I drove home across the toll bridge. It's quicker that way, and I wanted to get home as fast as I could. My foot pressed the accelerator, and I played a cassette loudly, to drown my feelings. Vivaldi. The only thing in the car. I would have preferred the Beatles. Or U2. Anything really loud and noisy.

What I felt was, of course, shame.

I didn't know if you'd heard or not. But, what if you had?

When I was crossing the bridge, I didn't have the forty pence in change, so I had to go to the kiosk. I handed in a pound, and when the man gave me the change, he placed in my hand one red rose.

I was overwhelmed.

I love surprises. I love free gifts. It was Valentine's Day, and I hadn't had a card, I hadn't had a flower. And now the man on the toll bridge was handing out roses, for free.

It lifted my heart.

I threw it on the seat, and when I got home and Jim opened the door I bowed and presented it to him with a flourish. As I was doing this, I noticed for the first time that it was not a real flower, as I had supposed at first, but one made of silk.

'That's all right, that's all right,' Jim reassured me, in his deep, consoling voice, his voice like a glass of warm milk. He uses it to placate me, to calm down the children, and it always works. Like magic. 'It's better than a real one. It'll last longer.'

I came into the hall. There was a smell of floor polish, and the whole house was clean and tidy. Often it's not. I'm not in control, I'm not a good housekeeper. Jim is. The girls were sitting at the kitchen table, eating sausages. I sat down with them, while Jim got a vase in the living room and put the rose in it.

It's still there. I can see it if I look over my shoulder right now. A red silk rose, in a blue glass vase.

You did hear, didn't you? I've known it all along, really. Although I did not become fully conscious of it until you were going back to Gothenburg. Then, I think, you told me, with your eyes. Or did you?

I would like to be sure of these things. How can I be sure?

Yes. Yes. I know you heard. And I want to thank you. That is what I am doing now. I'm writing to thank you, for being such a perfect gentleman.

Or do I? If I say, 'I want to rip you apart, for being a perfect gentleman,' that, too, would be true.

What is real about these sensations? What is real, one way or the other? Your shoes, the National Library? Your goodbye kiss? Your hand, brushing mine accidentally, for some seconds longer than necessary, as I passed the salt? The floor your shoe walks upon, is it that?

What I have now is not much. Some letters, never sent. A record, Sibelius. For which, thanks again. Oh, I do like Sibelius, when I'm in Clare, on the tops of the Cliffs of Moher, listening to the breakers breaking. In Dublin, he's not quite the thing, is he? But he's all I've got, of you.

What Jim has is a rose, made of cloth. Did I say, silk? Silk, indeed. It's some awful synthetic stuff, nylon or viscose, a cloth I hate more than any other in the whole world. A viscose rose in a Chinese vase, also fake.

The Catechism Examination

SOMETHING ABOUT the way the garden hedge looks today gives me a feeling I would have difficulty in describing, although I recognise it very well. I had this feeling before, as a child. Perhaps since then too. But I only recall the first time.

The hedge, let me say, is very still. A quiet, neat line, separating the garden from the road. At the far side of the road is a stone wall, and beyond that the sea, which is an even grey colour, with dark flecks where the waves dip. The sky is the same colour as the sea, only a little lighter. No seagulls, no garden birds, no dogs, are visible. Just lines, grey and dark grey and black. It is a foggy day, dull, and lovely.

We were to have our catechism examination. For three months, ever since the Christmas holidays, Miss

O'Byrne had been drilling us in the two-hundred-and-thirty questions we, as prospective First-Communicants, were expected to know. We learned five questions every night for the first two months, and then we revised ten a night during the month before the exam. Even the most stupid girl in the class, Mary Doyle, knew nearly all the answers by now.

Miss O'Byrne is a strict teacher. That is her reputation, what the big girls and the mothers say about her. And she lives up to it. She even looks strict: tall, with angular features and menacing butterfly glasses. The frames of her glasses are transparent, but the wings are brilliant royal blue, with diamonds glittering in the corners. Behind, above, her eyes sparkle, sharp and penetrating.

She strides in every morning, her thin legs pushing against her black pencil skirt. The first thing she does is call the roll. When a name is called and no one answers she glares at each face in turn, creating a palpable thrill of excitement in the big, Georgian drawing-room. Her eye rests, briefly, on me, and I feel afraid, and oddly pleased. Am I to be punished because, say, Mary Clarke is absent? She does not sit beside me, I have nothing much to do with her, I don't even like her. But Miss O'Byrne's ways are mysterious to me, and to all of us. Her system, if she has one, is not something we understand.

She looks down at the roll-book and we watch her fountain pen, a special Parker kept for performing this important task, scratch a big 'x' beside the name of the absentee. Miss O'Byrne smiles to herself, and shakes her head. Then she blots the roll-book with her pink blotter and the day begins.

Who made the world? Who is God? Who are the three persons of the Blessed Trinity? What is meant by Transubstantiation? What are the Ten Commandments? The Seven Deadly Sins? The Six Commandments of the Church?

Now, in the last week, she goes through all two-hundred-and-thirty questions every day. It takes from nine o'clock until two, given the half-hour break for lunch. She begins calmly, and the class, too, is calm, at first. The girls sit upright in their narrow desks, faces pink and newly scrubbed, hair brushed back and tied in blue ribbons. Gradually the pressure increases. Girls make mistakes, and have to stand out in line to be slapped. Three slaps for each mistake. Miss O'Byrne takes this part of the proceedings seriously. She slaps using three or four rulers, bound together with an elastic band. Rumour has it that she once tried to introduce a bamboo cane, but the Parents' Committee and the Parish Priest banned it: bamboo can leave marks.

Miss O'Byrne's patience goes, soon, and order vanishes. Girls grow hot and sweaty, waiting to be asked, hoping they will survive the day without punishment, although this hardly ever happens. Their faces become red, their white blouses grow black and floppy. Only Miss O'Byrne's sweater, white angora, remains immaculate, smelling of Mum and Dior.

She takes a break to teach us a moral lesson, to tell us about the Missions. Delighted to have a reprieve from the harrowing questioning, and eagerly anticipating the thrills to come, we sit up with suddenly renewed vigour in our desks. I run my fingers along the thick coarse grain of the wood: the wood is golden, and polished brilliantly by generations of woollen elbows, but the deep lines of its surface are filled with a black substance. It looks like fine clay, but it is dust. Ancient dust.

'Hands on your heads!' raps Miss O'Byrne, and we all obediently place our hands on the crowns of our heads. I feel my smooth hair, pulled tight downwards towards its pony tail. Underneath, my skin is hot and pulsating slightly.

The Missions. Nuns and priests and lay people who give up their lives to preach the word of God to pagans. Lay people, what are they? Some sort of hybrid, not fully human, I sense. People like Miss O'Byrne. Brave and unusual. They are killed. Tortured. She tells of pins under fingernails, tongues ripped out. I am not sure who does it, rips out the tongues. Communists, perhaps. Or black people. In Africa or China. Miss O'Byrne mentions South America but I have not heard of it before. Africa, I know all about Africa.

My arms are getting tired. I wish she would let us put them down again. When she does, the questioning will begin.

Nuns and priests and lay people are tortured, because they want to teach catechism to the pagans. And we can't learn ours properly. We are too lazy. Lazy, spoiled little city girls.

Mary Doyle is wrinkling up her face and moving her arms about dangerously. Stupid Mary Doyle. She can't learn, it seems, and she looks terrible. Small, scrawny, with thin blonde hair. Her face is white and sprinkled with freckles. Her gymslip hangs on her bony body.

She cries. Whenever she is punished, which is often, she bursts into huge uncontrollable sobs. Her pale face grows red and spotty, and her body shakes.

There is something wrong with Mary Doyle. I do not know what, but I have thought of her for some time and come to this conclusion. It irritates me, that she is on my mind. She is very often on my mind, because she is so strange, because there is something wrong with her. Why doesn't her mother do something about her?

Her mother is all right. I have seen her, sitting in the dark mildewed hall, under the statue of the Virgin: she wears a fawn teddy coat and inside her pink flowered headscarf her face is round and pleasant. Normal. Not skinny and odd. The trouble is, Mary's mother doesn't notice that her daughter is unusual. When Mary emerges from the cellar, where we hang our coats, Mrs Doyle gives her a kiss and says 'Hello lovey,' just like any other mother. Then Mary's face lights up as though there were a lamp underneath her transparent skin. And her mouth is really very big. She smiles and her whole face is taken over by the smile. She is like the Cheshire Cat my mummy reads about, at night in front of the fire in the kitchen. And even that, the way she lights up and turns into a smile, is odd. But Mrs Doyle just doesn't notice. She chats to the other mothers, about the price of First-Communion dresses and the French lessons we might get next year, as if Mary were the same as the other girls: solid, sturdy, in mind and body.

'Stop fidgeting, Mary Doyle,' says Miss O'Byrne. Mary's face wrinkles up and becomes pink. The bell rings, clanging violently through the cold gloomy rooms of the school. We are allowed to take down our hands. We are allowed to go down to the cellar, and out to our mothers, waiting in the hall.

Two days before the examination Miss O'Byrne is very nervous. Five pupils, five, are absent. During roll-call, her eyes dart about, stopping to rest for long periods now on one, now on another girl, daring those present to be absent tomorrow, or on the day of the examination itself. I feel genuinely frightened. I don't like Miss O'Byrne, but I have always trusted her not to go too far. She is an adult, she knows the limits. Today her eyes rest, for longer than is right, on me, and on others.

After roll-call, the test begins. It is a mock exam, a rehearsal for the real one, on Thursday. Tomorrow, Miss O'Byrne says, we will rest, and do no catechism. We do not believe her.

First she asks Monica Blennerhasset. Monica has thick glossy plaits, very white socks on slim legs, and a gym-slip which fits perfectly and is made of rich deep blue serge, not the black shiny stuff which wrinkles easily, the kind I have. Monica is the best pupil. Her father is a doctor and her mother president of the Parents' Committee, and she never misses. Usually I am disappointed when she is asked a question because the outcome is so certain, no risks involved. Now I am relieved.

Next, she asks me. I am not like Monica Blennerhasset, or Orla O'Connor, who is the prettiest girl in the class and a champion Irish dancer. She has tiny feet, which arch like a ballerina's in her little satin pumps — we call them 'poms'. She points them exquisitely to the floor, before leaping into a star rendering of 'The Hard Reel' or 'The Double Jig'. I am not like them, a certain winner. But I am not a loser, either, and as a rule I do well enough. I know the catechism, inside out. Mummy tests me every night, in front of the fire, before she reads *Alice in Wonderland*, before bed. I can recite the answers in my sleep. I know it so well that it bores me, and I am not afraid on my own account.

After me, it is Mary Doyle's turn. She trembles as she stands up. Oh, Mary Doyle, it's stupid to tremble! Her ribbon is loose, sliding down the back of her head.

'What is the meaning of the fourth commandment of the church?'

Mary begins: 'The meaning of the fourth commandment of the church is . . .' Then she stops. Miss O'Byrne repeats the question.

Mary repeats: 'The meaning of the fourth commandment of the . . . of the . . . of the . . .'

She is crying already.

'Stand out,' orders Miss O'Byrne, picking up her bunch of rulers.

My stomach tightens, and I feel a desire to laugh, which I suppress.

'Put out your hand.' The familiar formula has a novel quality.

Slap slap. The rulers bang together in the air, wood on wood. Then the loud smack of wood on flesh.

Six.

She would stop now.

Twelve.

Mary only missed one. Three for one. Mary is howling.

Fifteen.

Mary's sobbing has evened out, it is quieter.

Twenty.

I do not feel excited. I do not feel afraid. I want to get sick.

Twenty-three.

Mary is not howling at all. Her face is white. She is

falling onto the floor.

Miss O'Byrne touches her with her foot. She wears black patent shoes with stiletto heels, very high.

'Get up, Mary Doyle,' she raps, in her cross tone. Mary does not get up.

Miss O'Byrne glares at me. I sit in the front row.

'You. Get a glass of water.'

'Yes miss.'

I rise immediately and leave the room. A glass of water. I have never seen a glass in the school. We bring our own plastic mugs for lunch, and pour milk into them from ketchup bottles or green triangular cartons. In winter, Maggie, the woman who cleans, gives us hot water for cocoa. The teachers drink tea from delph cups: we see them, sitting in the Teachers' Room, which overlooks the yard. They sip tea, eat sandwiches from tinfoil wrappers, and talk, as they supervise our playing.

I decide that Maggie might be in the kitchen, and go down the stone stairs to the cellar, where it is situated in a cubby-hole beside the toilets. Luckily, I find her, hunched over a little coal fire, her worn-out navy overall wrapped tightly around her body. She regards me sadly, and doesn't speak, as she hands me a cup of water. The cup is white with a green rim, the kind of cup you get on trains, and it is sinewed with thousands of barely-visible veins, but it is neither cracked nor chipped.

'Did you go to the well?' Miss O'Byrne snaps. I make no response: I do not realise that her sarcasm, which is constant, is intended as humour.

Mary is sitting on a chair, her head between her knees. Thin fair hair droops onto the floorboards.

'Here, Mary, drink this.' Miss O'Byrne's voice is a catapult, the words tiny sharp stones.

Mary raises her head. Her face is whiter than ever, and her hand, when it reaches for the glass, is red, with blisters. But no blood.

'You did the ballet and passed out,' says Miss O'Byrne. Nobody knows what she is talking about.

I am standing beside Mary, waiting for the empty cup:

I hope that I may be allowed to return it to the kitchen. Idly, I put my hand in my pocket, and feel there a paper tube: it is a packet of fruit pastilles, which Mummy bought for me at Mrs Dunne's, the sweetshop in the lane behind the school. Without thinking, I take the packet and hand it to Mary. Miss O'Byrne does not see what I am doing.

Mary takes the sweets and puts them into her own pocket. She does not, of course, smile, but she looks at me with her bright green eyes, shiny from all the crying, rimmed with red skin. There is a light in them, though, that lamp she has inside. Ashamed and worried by my rashness, I sit down, forgetting about the cup. When Mary stops drinking, Miss O'Byrne puts it on her table, and it is still there at two o'clock as the bell clangs and we file out to the hall.

On Thursday we are allowed to wear our own clothes. I have a red dress, nylon, with white spots. Underneath is a red silk slip, and underneath that a crinoline of stiff net, which scratches my legs but makes the skirt stand out like a lampshade, which is exactly the effect I desire.

All the girls wear their best dresses. Pink and lemon and sky blue. They all have crinolines, but nobody else has a red dress. Mummy made it for me herself, because red suits me so well.

There is an air of great excitement in the classroom, engendered by the party dresses and the prospect of the examination. Girls giggle and scream. Miss O'Byrne, in a navy suit with an emerald-green blouse, bangs her rulers against the desk, but cannot maintain order, because she has to keep running in and out of the office, talking to the other teachers, and wondering when the priest will come.

Fr Harpur arrives at half past ten. His hair is grey and curly, and his face soft. On his cheek is a brown spot, a kind of mole, and when he speaks his voice is very quiet and gentle.

'Hello, girls,' he says, gazing around with a smile. 'I'm sure you know your catechism very well indeed by now. Do you know, a little bird told me, that you are all very good girls, and know everything in the catechism. Is that true?'

Monica Blennerhasset smiles broadly and says, 'Yes, Father.' Some of the others nod.

'Now, I'm going to ask you something very hard, but very important. Can anyone recite the "Our Father"?'

We are taken aback, for a moment. The 'Our Father' isn't even in the catechism. But all hands shoot up, and some are waved about, eagerly. He asks Orla O'Connor, who had nodded to his first question. She says the prayer in a slow, considered voice, not the kind of tone we use for real catechism.

'Very good. The Lord's Prayer. It is a beautiful prayer, the Lord's Prayer. Jesus himself taught it to us. Jesus who loved little children, "Suffer the little children to come unto me," he said, didn't he?'

Nobody bothers to reply.

'Will you promise me something, girls?'

We nod.

'Will you promise me to say the Lord's Prayer every day for the rest of your lives?'

'Yes, Father,' we say, in our subdued voices, which probably sound pious to him.

'Very good. And now, since you are all such good girls, and know your catechism so well, I think you should have a half-day. What do you say, Miss O'Byrne?'

'Whatever you say, Fr Harpur,' she says, her voice polite and respectful. She gives us a beaming smile, and we get up and file out. We knew we would get a half-day. The big girls told us about it. Miss O'Byrne warned the mothers, who are waiting, in the hall, under the statue of the Virgin.

'Well, how did you get on?' Mummy asks.

'Oh, all right,' I say. 'The priest was nice.' But I do not like the priest. I do not like him at all.

Instead of going home, we went to the Spring Show. It

was my first time, and Ladies' Day. I recall it vividly. The hats. The free samples of flavoured milk and garlic sausage. The combine-harvesters. And the sound of the horses' feet, pounding, pounding, against the fragrant turf in the enclosure. It was a calm April day. Dull and poignant with the promise of summer. Like today.

The Duck-Billed Platypus

'MIND IF I smoke?'

Joseph Dale lifted his eyes from the foreign affairs page of the national daily in response to the flat Dublin accent.

'Not at all. Go right ahead.'

The second contender for the Civil Service appointment was firmly seated in a corner of the grey room. Fair hair, red dress, thick ankles: she'd make a good diplomat, he reflected. The auntie-image, so dear to all hearts at home and on overseas service. No scandals there anyway. And he pushed aside the newspaper bitterly. Nothing it could teach him; he had read all the reports, all the surveys, all the journals, white papers, pink pamphlets, histories. He knew the set-up. Inside-out. Had it all weighed up. Knew why he should get this job. Knew why he hadn't a chance from the word go.

So he stared at a ray of sunshine dancing on the wall.

ACADEMIC VIEW OF THE JOB CRISIS

'You *are* going to go ahead and apply?'
'Well, yes.'
'Oh, it's a good idea, you know, a really good idea. The experience will do you all the good in the world. No harm in getting to know the, eh, the set-up.'
'I thought it would be a good idea . . . the interview . .'
'What do you in fact consider to be your prospects?'
'Well, I'm not very hopeful. My qualifications aren't exactly suited to the job, and I'm not sure that I'd enjoy it anyway.'
'Ye-es. Your subjects are hardly in their line; economics or something might have been more relevant.'
'They do like to have some literary people on the staff, I'm told.'
'Of course. Of course. Of course. Of course . . .'
Damned idiot.

The girl in the corner swished her dress against the plastic seat. Synthetic silk on synthetic plastic. Cacophonous synthesis grated on his whole system. Opposition tactics. He loathed the girl. Not that she would get the job either. But he hated to belong to the same crumby set as her, the set of the unsmart-highly-educated-contending-for-anything-that's-going set, the dice-loaded-against-us-from-the-start set.
'Would you care for a chocolate?' The sing-song tones again.
'Oh no thanks.' He was astonished. Sweets at an interview. Definitely news. 'I never eat sweets.'
She began to munch. The sugar of life.

SWEET FACTORY CLOSES DOWN

Owing to a drastic decline in the national consumption of confectionery Bon-bon Bros. Ltd. of Rock Kandy Mt. have been forced to close their factory. One hundred jobless sweet-makers will join the dole queues as a result.

What do you know? No jobs on the bon-bon belt. But I've lost a hundred jobs already, all by myself. A hundred thousand more to lose. They slip away, rosy apples to the cider-heap, red plums to rot in the basket; a hundred thousand nests and niches whence I should contribute to society past and future melt from me.

PORTER USHERS HOPELESS CASE TO INTERVIEW BOARD

'Joseph Dale?'.

Waxen-faced with a puckered moustache. Black suited, the porter looked like a punctuation mark against the grey walls. Question or expletive? Laughing policeman. But his voice had the charm of a funeral dirge freezing his quaking guts.

'Would you come this way please?'

Joseph Dale followed the black porter into the dry vaulted chamber. Behind the oval table sat three figures, whom close inspection revealed to be two male and one female. They affixed him with a triplicate quizzical look. He stared back blankly. After two minutes the males began to leaf through sheaves of papers. The female attacked.

'We'll have a little look at your curriculum vitae first, just to warm up.' (She was an old bird, lightly thatched). She motioned towards a list of dates.

'So you went to school in St. James', Cambridge Hill?'

Cambridge Hill N.S. has wire netting on the window and broken basket-ball nets in the yard and teachers with walloping rulers in the class-rooms. I spent my youth avoiding being clobbered. A cowardly little boy indeed.

'I attended the primary school there for eight years.'

'And then you moved to Mount Styan?'

'Mount Styan. I was there for six years, until I was seventeen.'

The lady looked extremely bored and tired. Tell her only what she wants to hear or she'll drop dead from exhaustion.

In Mount Styan I learned about LIFE from inebriates and morons: no.

'And you got six honours in your Leaving. What were your best subjects then?'

'Physics and English.'

I cheated on the Physics paper. That's why I got an A on it and a B in English. Formulae written on the back of my tie. Good trick. Never fails. Everyone does it. Conform or you're lost: that's what Mount Styan taught me.

The woman's job is to probe the personality. To psyche me out. To judge my reactions. Should they be stronger? Am I emerging as a literary bore? A drink of water?

Through his mind floated the vague notion of telling a blatant lie. A laugh for afterwards over the inevitable pint. Her bead-eyes would twitch and water in surprise and he would mock her face. He would say: 'My favourite subjects were the Seven Deadlies: Sex, Communism, Mother-beating, Blasphemy, Apathy, The Bottle and Poetry.' A bit weak. Try again.

'My favourite subject was English Literature.'

'Yes. I see. A B, and what did you do then?'

'I took a degree in English.'

'And what did you consider to be your career prospects when you undertook this course of study?'

You know the answer to that one, (you withered old crow). I considered: after the rut of Mount Styan the joy of the liberated days, the exploration of the writing of the world, general recognition and acceptance of my personal brilliance in every field, academic and otherwise, the falling of the world at my feet. I knew, in short, dear lady, that I had more in my brain than anyone in the university just as you knew too before you ended up in this cushy soul-murdering job, to sit on a poker and interview zombies.

'I considered the possibility of an academic career, as a teacher.'

'And have you entirely discarded this idea?'

Her winged eyes gimlet you. Please now watch the

birdie. Phrase the answer with care or you've had it. On your mark . . .

'To be perfectly honest . . .'

Get set . . .

'I have not discarded it entirely. My interest has been . . .'

Ah, that's the spirit, boy. More of the same . . .

'Always in a literary area. My hope is to ultimately fulfil this interest in a suitable career. But you understand the difficulty I encounter in acquiring such a position during the present economic crisis.'

Made it, baby. Watch her drool. Done it again, so be glad and rejoice.

'Of course. Well. Now. I'll pass you on to Mr Cripps.'

Mr Cripps, whiskey nosed, fat and fleshy. Jeremiah Cripps. Gives kiddies the creeps when he walks down the road on air-cushioned soles every morning at nine rising to shine like sun on the water. Cut the rhetoric. Cut.

'Mr Dale: these societies to which you belong, the Rathmines Otters, the English Lit., the Mountain Ramblers, the Maths. Society, and all the rest of them . . .'

The Football Flies, Macra na Feirme, the Doomsday Bunch, Rogues, the Parliament of Fools, the Church of Ireland . . .

'How can you possibly keep up with them all?'

Well of course I don't keep up with them all, Mr Cripps, you examiner of the social and popular. I don't keep up with them at all at all. Bless me Jeremiah for I have just put them down on the list for the crack. I hated every one of them right from the start when I saw the canker at the heart of the structure. The hierarchy of President, Secretary, Treasurer, guardians of the moral spirits and manners of ordinary member shrivelled under my worm-gnawing gaze as soon as I had attended the first meeting. I knew before that, always, born as I was with the worm of vision. The happy sepulchres danced and spilled and sucked me to them but the worm stayed in me. No mindless fun for me, Jeremiah, you founder-member of every society in the world, you creep, you.

'In my initial year at college, my level of involvement was intense: I audited the Maths. Society, and was treasurer of the English Lit.'

'And since then?'

'Gradually, my interest in social life was superseded by an interest in work.'

'Ah, yes.' Mr Cripps lit up with comprehension. Squandered the splendid years, had he, for work-interest? Stupid? Hardly. Blind?

'And your interest in sport? The Otters? Football?'

Are you sound in body if not in mind?

'Swimming is my . . .'

Risk it. The human touch.

'. . . passion. I was the best swimmer in the Otters.'

'You competed then?'

What did I fish up from the otter pool? What metallic trophy on the side-board to prove me a fish in the black water? In the dark water I follow the red centre of my sight. The red light sucks me in. The fish. Nobody catches me with metallic nasty hooks.

But Jeremiah, you walker on water, you have me now. The game is up.

'I preferred not to compete. My interest was in swimming rather than in competition.'

'Ah, yes. Of course.' Jeremiah Cripps, walker on water, reeled him in.

'Well, perhaps, Mr O'Dowd?'

Garret O'Dowd was the picture of all that thrives in western society. Garret O'Dowd adjust the all-encompassing non-corruptible frame of your *pince-nez* and show me my sin. That scald-crow in the corner, the holy shrike, has failed to even pin-point the canker. The man of flesh disturbed my soil and stirred it up. Now move in and see what you can find, Mr O'Dowd. For the kill. Dissect the worm: make a section for me on a gold-rimmed slide.

'So, Mr Dale. Your work-interest superseded your interest in social activities, did it? Was there a reason for this?'

The neon-red wound was so bright and strong. It drew me in. From the monotony of days, of orders, of people, the interminable ranks of hours and minds. Structures so rigid. Only the glorious red fuse, the formless sight, could satisfy my craving. Ultimate blindness and sight. And to hell with social activities.

'By reading, I learned more about life than I could have learned from people.'

Mr O'Dowd's nose twitched slightly. His eyes widened.

'Do you honestly think so, Mr Dale?'

Sock it to them, for Christ's sake.

'I've always known it.'

The crow-woman in the corner fluttered her wide-winged eyes. Jeremiah Cripps raised a pudgy hand in a gesture of wonder.

'Ah. Of course. Mr Dale,' said Mr O'Dowd, bland as nothing on earth.

'So why,' asked Mr Garret O'Dowd, 'do you feel suited to the job in the diplomatic service?'

I don't want this job in the diplomatic service. I'm not a diplomatic jarvey, an international butler. I can't abide the ranks and orders, the eternal trinities. I am not a robot like you and all the other humans I have ever met. Conform and survive: the lesson of Mount Styan. I have learned a new trick since my Mount Styan days.

The three interviewers observed with close concern the face of the young man, the common face of the arty type they had encountered so often before. Joseph Dale considered giving either of the following replies:

'I am a quick learner. I can organise easily. I am willing to do all you ask.'

or

'I don't have the qualifications. I don't want the job. Let me get the hell out of here from your rotten sacred organisation.'

Joseph answered:

'I don't know.'

'Ah. You don't know. Mr Dale.' The bland eye of

Garret O'Dowd pierced him.

'You don't know?' Jeremiah Cripps stared him down.

'You don't know, Mr Dale?' The bird-woman fluttered again.

They surround me with chalk-white faces, spearing my soul. They are robbing my light, not finding the worm, just stealing my glowing red light, the centre of my putrid universe. Stupid statues of chalk, I am not of your kind.

'Well goodbye, Mr Dale. Thank you for coming in.'

They damn me thus. Am I impervious? Protect me, red glow. Electrify me. Vivify me.

'Goodbye.'

He retreated unsteadily from the ordeal, one more misfit over the brink. The sweet plump girl swished past him, stiletto heels clicking belligerently against the tiled floor. A strong sticky smell, of musk or roses, lingered in her wake, as she marched across the threshold to face the Board.

Blood and Water

I HAVE an aunt who is not the full shilling. 'The Mad Aunt' was how my sister and I referred to her when we were children, but that was just a euphemism, designed to shelter us from the truth which we couldn't stomach: she was mentally retarded. Very mildly so: perhaps she was just a slow learner. She survived very successfully as a lone farm woman, letting land, keeping a cow and a few hens and ducks, listening to the local gossip from the neighbours who were kind enough to drop in regularly in the evenings. Quite a few of them were: her house was a popular place for callers, and perhaps that was part of the secret of her survival. She did not participate in the neighbours' conversation to any extent, however. She was articulate only on a very concrete level, and all abstract topics were beyond her.

Had she been born in the fifties or sixties, my aunt would have been scientifically labelled, given special treatment at a special school, taught special skills and eventually employed in a special workshop to carry out a special job, certainly a much duller job than the one she pursued in reality. Luckily for her she was born in 1925 and had been reared as a normal child. Her family had failed to recognise that she was different from others and had not sought medical attention for her. She had merely been considered 'delicate'. The term 'mentally retarded' would have been meaningless in those days, anyway, in the part of Donegal where she and my mother originated, where Irish was the common, if not the only, language. As she grew up, it must have been silently conceded that she was a little odd. But people seemed to have no difficulty in suppressing this fact, and they judged my aunt by the standards which they applied to humanity at large: sometimes lenient and sometimes not.

She lived in a farmhouse in Ballytra on Inishowen, and once a year we visited her. Our annual holiday was spent under her roof. And had it not been for the lodging she provided, we could not have afforded to get away at all. But we did not consider this aspect of the affair.

On the first Saturday of August we always set out, laden with clothes in cardboard boxes and groceries from the cheap city shops, from the street markets: enough to see us through the fortnight. The journey north lasted nearly twelve hours in our ancient battered cars: a Morris Eight, dark green with fragrant leather seats, and a Ford Anglia are two of the models I remember from a long series of fourth-hand crocks. Sometimes they broke down en route and caused us long delays in nauseating garages, where I stood around with my father, while the mechanic tinkered, or went, with my sister and mother, for walks down country lanes, or along the wide melancholy street of small market towns.

Apart from such occasional hitches, however, the trips were delightful odysseys through various flavours of Ireland: the dusty rich flatlands outside Dublin, the drumlins of Monaghan with their hint of secrets and better things to come, the luxuriant slopes, rushing rivers and expensive villas of Tyrone, and finally, the ultimate reward: the furze and heather, the dogroses, the fuchsia, of Donegal.

Donegal was different in those days. Different from what it is now, different then from the eastern urban parts of Ireland. It was rural in a thorough, elemental way. People were old-fashioned in their dress and manners, even in their physiques: weather-beaten faces were highlighted by black or grey suits, shiny with age; broad hips stretched the cotton of navy-blue, flower-sprigged overalls, a kind of uniform for country women which their city sisters had long eschewed, if they ever had it. Residences were thatched cottages ... 'the Irish peasant house' ... or spare grey farmhouses. There was only a single bungalow in the parish where my aunt lived, an area which is now littered with them.

All these things accentuated the rusticity of the place, its strangeness, its uniqueness.

My aunt's house was of the slated, two-storey variety, and it stood, surrounded by a seemingly arbitrary selection of outhouses, in a large yard called 'the street'. Usually we turned into this street at about nine o'clock at night, having been on the road all day. My aunt would be waiting for us, leaning over the half-door. Even though she was deaf, she would have heard the car while it was still a few hundred yards away, chugging along the dirt lane: it was always that kind of car. She would stand up as soon as we appeared, and twist her hands shyly, until we emerged from the car. Then she would walk slowly over to us, and shake hands carefully with each of us in turn, starting with my mother. Care, formality: these were characteristics which were most obvious in her. Slowness.

Greetings over, we would troop into the house, under a low portal apparently designed for a smaller race of people. Then we would sit in front of the hot fire, and my mother would talk, in a loud cheery voice, telling my aunt the news from Dublin and asking for local gossip. My aunt would sometimes try to reply, more often not. After five minutes or so of this, she would indicate, a bit resentfully, that she had expected us earlier, that she had been listening for the car for over two days. And my mother, still, at this early stage of the holiday, in a diplomatic mood, would explain patiently, slowly, loudly, that no, we had been due today. We always came on the first Saturday, didn't we? John only got off on the Friday, sure. But somehow my mother would never have written to my aunt to let her know when we were coming. It was not owing to the fact that the latter was illiterate that she didn't write. Any neighbour would have read a letter for her. It was, rather, the result of a strange convention which my parents, especially my mother, always adhered to: they never wrote to anyone, about anything, except one subject. Death.

While this courteous ritual of fireside conversation was being enacted by my parents (although in fact my father never bothered to take part), my sister and I would sit silently on our hardbacked chairs, fidgeting and looking at the familiar objects in the room: the Sacred Heart, the Little Flower, the calendar from Bells of Buncrana depicting a blond laughing child, the red arc for layers' mash. We answered promptly, monosyllabically, the few questions my aunt put to us, all concerning school. Subdued by the immense boredoms of the day, we tolerated further boredom.

After a long time, my mother would get up, stretch, and prepare a meal of rashers and sausages, from Russells of Camden Street. To this my aunt would add a few provisions she had laid in for us: eggs, butter she had churned herself, and soda bread which she baked in a pot oven, in enormous golden balls. I always refused to eat this bread, because I found the taste repellent and because I didn't think my aunt washed her hands properly. My sister, however, ate no other kind of bread while we were on holiday at that house, and I used to tease her about it, trying to force her to see my point of view. She never did.

After tea, although by that time it was usually late, we would run outside and play. We would visit each of the outhouses in turn, hoping to see an owl in the barn and then we'd run across the road to a stream which flowed behind the back garden. There was a stone bridge over the stream and on our first night we invariably played the same game: we threw sticks into the stream at one side of the bridge, and then ran as fast as we could to the other side in order to catch them as they sailed out. This activity, undertaken at night in the shadow of the black hills, had a magical effect: it plummetted me headlong into the atmosphere of the holidays. At that stream, on that first night, I would suddenly discover within myself a feeling of happiness and freedom that I was normally unaware I possessed. It seemed to emerge from some hidden part of me, like the sticks emerging from underneath the bridge, and it counteracted the faint claustrophobia, the nervousness, which I always had initially in my aunt's house.

Refreshed and elated, we would go to bed in unlit upstairs rooms. These bedrooms were panelled in wood which had been white once, but had faded to the colour of butter, and they had windows less than two feet square which had to be propped up with a stick if you wanted them to remain open: the windows were so small, my mother liked to tell us, because they had been made at a time when there was a tax on glass. I wondered about this: the doors were tiny, too.

When I woke up in the morning, I would lie and count the boards on the ceiling, and then the knots on the boards, until eventually a clattering of footsteps on the uncarpeted stairs and a banging about of pots and pans would announce that my mother was up and that breakfast would soon be available. I would run downstairs to the scullery, which served as a bathroom, and wash. The basin stood on a deal table, the water was in a white enamel bucket on the dresser. A piece of soap was stuck to a saucer on the window-sill, in front of the basin: through the window, you could see a bit of an elm tree, and a purple hill, as you washed.

In a way it was pleasant, but on the whole it worried me, washing in that place. It was so public. There was a constant danger that someone would rush in, and find you there, half undressed, scrubbing your armpits. I liked my ablutions to be private and unobserved.

The scullery worried me for another reason. On its wall, just beside the dresser, was a big splodge of a dirty yellow substance, unlike anything I had ever encountered. I took it to be some sort of fungus. God knows why, since the house was unusually clean. This thing so repelled me that I never even dared to ask what it was, and simply did my very best to avoid looking at it while I was in its vicinity, washing or bringing back the bucket of water from the well, or doing anything else. Years later, when I was taking a course in ethnology at the university, I realised that the stuff was nothing other than butter, daubed on the wall after every churning, for luck. But to me it symbolised something quite other than good fortune, something unthinkably horrible.

After dressing, breakfast. Rashers and sausages again, fried over the fire by my mother, who did all the cooking while we were on holiday. For that fortnight my aunt, usually a skilful frier of rashers, baker of bread, abdicated domestic responsibility to her, and adopted the role of child in her own house, like a displaced rural mother-in-law. She spent her time fiddling around in the henhouse, feeding the cat, or more often she simply sat, like a man, and stared out of the window while my mother worked. After about three days of this, my mother would grow resentful, would begin to mutter, gently but persistently, 'it's no holiday!' And my sister and I, even though we understood the reasons for our aunt's behaviour, as, indeed, did our mother, would nod in agreement. Because we had to share in the housework. We set the table, we did the washing up in an enamel basin, and I had personal responsibility for going to the well to draw water. For this, my sister envied me. She imagined it to be a privileged task, much more fun than sweeping or making beds. And of course it was more exotic than these chores, for the first day or so, which was why I insisted on doing it. But soon enough the novelty palled, and it was really hard work, and boring. Water is heavy, and we seemed to require a great deal of it.

Unlike our mother, we spent much time away from the kitchen, my sister and I. Most of every morning we passed on the beach. There was an old boathouse there, its roof almost caved in, in which no boat had been kept for many many years. It had a stale smell, faintly disgusting, as if animals, or worse, had used it as a lavatory at some stage in the past. Even though the odour dismayed us, and even though the beach was always quite deserted, we liked to undress in private, both of us together, and therefore going to great lengths with towels to conceal our bodies from one another, until such a time as we should emerge from the yawning door of the building, and run down the golden quartz slip into the sea.

Lough Swilly. Also known as 'The Lake of Shadows', my sister often informed me, this being the type of fact of which she was very fond. One of the only two fjords in Ireland, she might also add. That meant nothing to me, its being a fjord, and as for shadows, I was quite unaware of them. What I remember most about that water is its crystal clarity. It was greenish, to look at it from a slight distance. Or, if you looked at it from my aunt's house, on a fine day, it was a brilliant turquoise colour, it looked like a great jewel, set in the hills. But when you were in that water, bathing, it was as clear as glass: I would swim along with my face just below the lapping surface, and I would open my eyes and look right down to the sandy floor, at the occasional starfish, the tiny crabs that scuttled there, at the shoals of minnows that scudded from place to place, guided by some mysterious mob instinct. I always stayed in for ages, even on the coldest days, even when rain was falling in soft curtains around the rocks. It had a definite benign quality, that water. And I always emerged from it cleansed in both body and soul. When I remember it now, I can understand why rivers are sometimes believed to be holy. Lough Swilly was, for me, a blessed water.

The afternoons we spent *en famille*, going on trips in the car to view distant wonders, Portsalon or the Downings. And the evenings we would spend 'raking', dropping in on our innumerable friends and drinking tea and playing with them.

This pattern continued for the entire holiday, with two exceptions: on one Sunday we would go on a pilgrimage to Doon Well, and on one weekday we would go to Derry, thirty miles away, to shop.

Doon Well was my aunt's treat. It was the one occasion, apart from Mass, on which she accompanied us on a drive, even though we all realised that she would have liked to be with us every day. But the only outing she insisted upon was Doon Well. She would begin to hint about it gently soon after we arrived. 'The Gallaghers were at Doon Well on Sunday,' she might say. 'Not a great crowd at it!' Then on Sunday she would not change her clothes after Mass, but would don a special elegant apron, and perform the morning tasks in a particular and lady-like way: tiptoe into the byre, flutter at the hens.

At two we would set out, and she would sit with me and my sister in the back of the car. My sense of mortification, at being seen in public with my aunt, was mixed with another shame, that of ostentatious religious practices. I couldn't bear processions, missions, concelebrated masses: display. At heart, I was Protestant, and indeed it would have suited me, in more ways than one, to belong to that faith. But I didn't. So I was going to Doon Well, with my aunt and my unctuous parents, and my embarrassed sister.

You could spot the well from quite a distance: it was dressed. In rags. A large assembly of sticks, to which brightly coloured scraps of cloth were tied, advertised its presence and lent it a somewhat flippant, pagan air. But it was not flippant, it was all too serious. As soon as we left the safety of the car, we had to remove our shoes. The pain! Not only of going barefoot on the stony ground, but of having to witness feet, adult feet, our parents' and our aunt's, so shamelessly revealed to the world. Like all adults then, their feet were horrible: big and yellow, horny with corns and ingrown toenails, twisted and tortured by years of ill-fitting boots, no boots at all. To crown it, both my mother and aunt had varicose veins, purple knots bulging hideously through the yellow skin. As humiliated as anyone could be, and as we were meant to be, no doubt, we had to circle the well some specified number of times, probably three, and we had to say the Rosary, out loud, in the open air. And then my mother had a long litany to Colmcille, to which we had to listen and respond, in about a thousand agonies of shame, 'Pray for us!' The only tolerable part of the expedition occurred immediately after this, when we bought souvenirs at a stall, with a gay striped awning more appropriate to Bray or Bundoran than to this grim place. There we stood and scrutinized the wares on display: beads, statuettes, medals, snowstorms. Reverting to our consumerist role, we . . . do I mean I? I assume my sister felt the same about it all . . . felt almost content, for a few minutes, and we always selected the same souvenirs, namely snowstorms. I have one still: it has a painted blue backdrop, now peeling a little, and figures of elves and mushrooms under the glass, and, painted in black letters on its wooden base, 'I have prayed for you at Doon Well.' I bought that as a present for my best friend, Ann Byrne, but when I returned to Dublin I hadn't the courage to give it to her so it stayed in my bedroom for years, until I moved to Germany to study, and then I brought it with me. As a souvenir, not of Doon Well, I think, but of something.

We went to Derry without my aunt. We shopped and ate sausages and beans for lunch, in Woolworths. I enjoyed the trip to Derry. It was the highlight of the holiday, for me.

At the end of the fortnight, we would shake hands with my aunt in the street, and say goodbye. On these occasions her face would grow long and sad, she would always, at the moment when we climbed into the car, actually cry quietly to herself. My mother would say: 'Sure we won't feel it now till it's Christmas! And then the summer will be here in no time at all!' And this would make everything much more poignant for my aunt, for me, for everyone. I would squirm on the seat, and, although I often wanted to cry myself, not because I was leaving my aunt but because I didn't want to give up the countryside, and the stream, and the clean clear water, I wouldn't think of my own unhappiness, but instead divert all my energy into despising my aunt for breaking yet another taboo: grown-ups do not cry.

My sister was tolerant. She'd laugh kindly as we turned out of the street onto the lane. 'Poor old Annie!' she'd say. But I couldn't laugh, I couldn't forgive her at all, for crying, for being herself, for not being the full shilling.

There was one simple reason for my hatred, so simple that I understood it myself, even when I was eight or nine years old. I resembled my aunt physically. 'You're the image of your Aunt Annie!', people, relations, would beam at me as soon as I met them, in the valley. Now I know, looking at photos of her, looking in the glass, that this was not such a very bad thing. She had a reasonable enough face, as faces go. But I could not see this when I was a child, much less when a teenager. All I knew then was that she looked wrong. For one thing, she had straight unpermed hair, cut short across the nape of the neck, unlike the hair of any woman I knew then (but quite like mine as it is today). For another, she had thick unplucked eyebrows, and no lipstick or powder, even on Sunday, even for Doon Well. Although at that time it was unacceptable to be unmade up, it was outrageous to wear straight hair and laced shoes. Even in a place which was decidedly old-fashioned, she looked uniquely outmoded. She looked, to my city-conditioned eyes, like a freak. So when people would say to me, 'God, aren't you the image of your auntie!' I would cringe and wrinkle up in horror. Unable to change my own face, and unable to see that it resembled hers in the slightest . . . and how does a face that is ten resemble one that is fifty? . . . I grew to hate my physique. And I transferred that hatred, easily and inevitably, to my aunt.

When I was eleven, and almost finished with family holidays, I visited Ballytra alone, not to stay with my aunt, but to attend an Irish college which had just been established in that district. I did not stay with any of my many relatives, on purpose: I wanted to steer clear of all unecessary contact with my past, and lived with a family I had never seen before.

Even though I loved the rigorous jolly ambiance of the college, it posed problems for me. On the one hand, I was the child of one of the natives of the parish, I was almost a native myself. On the other hand, I was what was known there as a 'scholar', one of the kids from Dublin or Derry who descended on Ballytra like a shower of fireworks in July, who acted as if they owned the place, who more or less shunned the native population.

If I'd wanted to, it would have been very difficult for me to steer a median course between my part as a 'scholar' and my other role, as a cousin of the little native 'culchies' who, if they had been my playmates in former years, were now too shabby, too rustic, too outlandish, to tempt me at all. In the event, I made no effort to play to both factions: I managed by ignoring my relations entirely, and throwing myself into the more appealing life of the 'scholar'. My relations, I might add, seemed not to notice this, or care, if they did, and no doubt they were as bound by their own snobberies and conventions as I was by mine.

When the weather was suitable, that is, when it did not rain heavily, afternoons were spent on the beach, the same beach upon which my sister and I had always played. Those who wanted to swim walked there, from the school, in a long straggling crocodile. I loved to swim and never missed an opportunity to go to the shore.

The snag about this was that it meant passing by my aunt's house, which was on the road down to the lough:

we had to pass through her street to get there. For the first week, she didn't bother me, probably assuming that I would drop in soon. But, even though my mother had warned me to pay an early visit and had given me a head-scarf to give her, I procrastinated. So after a week had gone by she began to lie in wait for me: she began to sit on her stone seat, in front of the door, and to look at me dolefully as I passed. And I would give a little casual nod, such as I did to everyone I met, and pass on.

One afternoon, the teacher who supervised the group was walking beside me and some of my friends, much to my pride and discomfiture. When we came to the street, she called, softly, as I passed, 'Mary, Mary'. I nodded and continued on my way. The teacher gave me a funny look and said: 'Is she talking to you, Mary? Does she want to talk to you?' 'I don't know her,' I said, melting in shame. 'Who is she?' 'Annie, that's Annie Bonner.' He didn't let on to know anything more about it, but I bet he did: everyone who had spent more than a day in Ballytra knew everything there was to know about it, everyone, that is, who wasn't as egocentric as the 'scholars'.

My aunt is still alive, but I haven't seen her in many years. I never go to Inishowen now. I don't like it since it became modern and littered with bungalows. Instead I go to Barcelona with my husband, who is a native Catalonian. He teaches Spanish here, part-time, at the university, and runs a school for Spanish students in Ireland during the summers. I help him in the tedious search for digs for all of them, and really we don't have much time to holiday at all.

My aunt is not altogether well. She had a heart attack just before Christmas and had to have a major operation at the Donegal Regional. I meant to pay her a visit, but never got around to it. Then, just before she was discharged, I learned that she was going home for Christmas. Home? To her own empty house, on the lane down to the lough? I was, to my surprise, horrified. God knows why, I've seen people in direr straits. But something gave. I phoned my mother and wondered angrily why she wouldn't have her, just for a few weeks. But my mother is getting on, she has gout, she can hardly walk herself. So I said, 'All right, she can come here!' But Julio was unenthusiastic. Christmas is the only time of the year he manages to relax: in January, the bookings start, the planning, the endless meetings and telephone calls. Besides, he was expecting a guest from home: his sister, Montserrat, who is tiny and dark and lively as a sparrow. The children adore her. In the end, my sister, unmarried and a lecturer in Latin at Trinity, went to stay for a few weeks in Ballytra until my aunt was better. She has very flexible holidays, my sister, and no real ties.

I was relieved, after all, not to have Aunt Annie in my home. What would my prim suburban neighbours have thought? How would Julio, who has rather aristocratic blood, have coped? I am still ashamed, you see, of my aunt. I am still ashamed of myself. Perhaps, I suspect, I do resemble her, and not just facially. Perhaps there is some mental likeness too. Are my wide education, my brilliant husband, my posh accent, just attempts at camouflage? Am I really all that bright? Sometimes, as I sit and read in my glass-fronted bungalow, looking out over the clear sheet of the Irish Sea, and try to learn something, the grammar of some foreign language, the names of Hittite gods, something like that, I find the facts running away from me, like sticks escaping downstream on the current. And more often than that, much more often, I feel in my mind a splodge of something that won't allow any knowledge to sink in. A block of some terrible substance, soft and thick and opaque. Like butter.

Tandoori

'SHE'S EXTREMELY good at physics. I think that's significant, don't you? I mean, if you're good at physics you're good at everything. You're just plain clever. Don't you agree?'

Karen, her hair falling over her shoulders like wisps of old straw, trapped me with gleaming eyes from her side of the table.

'Yes. Oh yes. I do.'

'That's really why I think it's so important that she switches to St. Matilda's. If she weren't so clever it wouldn't matter so much. But she'd benefit so much from a better environment. Better teaching. I'm convinced of it. And they're so marvellous. You can sense the . . .'

The waiter crept up behind me, armed with a battery of stainless-steel dishes. A white cloth trailed from his right arm.

'Everything O.K., sir?' he grinned in that obsequious way they often have. It always reminds me that the Empire still exists. No longer out there across the waves, but all around us, in their land, in ours. Right here in Dun Laoghaire. Should I say Kingstown?

'Yes.'

I felt a strong desire to answer rudely. Sometimes I find that soft brown-skinned courtesy charming. And at other times, such as the time in question, I want to seize the Indian by the scruff of the neck and shake all that jarveyish submission out of him. Even though I know perfectly well it's not genuine. Just a professional veneer, traditional shrewd superficiality. Its shrewdness doesn't make it more palatable, of course. Prostitution of anything, even of commonplace politeness, is never pleasant.

'It was lovely,' Karen gushed. What a convincing gush she has! 'Always lovely!' Then, she does enjoy the junk.

He broadened his smile, inclined his head almost to a bow, and arranged fresh offerings on the altar. Yellow rice, red chicken, green lettuce. Unleavened bread in a hand-plaited rush basket added the final touch of ceremony. He placed it lovingly in the centre of the table, nodded his black mop and sneaked away.

Karen helped herself.

'I love this bread. I adore it. I wonder how on earth they make it? Perhaps if I asked they'd give me the recipe. What do you think?'

'I daresay they would.' I smiled, possibly for the first time since we had arrived in the 'Taj Mahal' half an hour earlier. I had had a difficult week. My sales had been down for July and August and I had felt obliged to make a special effort to boost them during the past week. I had met hundreds of prospective customers, driving all over Leinster in the sticky September heat. I am a traveller for Teddy Bums, disposable babies' nappies.

'Mm, it is delicious, isn't it? It never fails, Indian cookery, properly done. I would so much like to do a little myself. But it hardly seems worth it, when one can just come here. Still, I love to cook. I think that's why the girls don't cook, don't you? They do other things, but they're never in the kitchen. They can't boil an egg, even, actually.'

She lapsed into silence, pondering this mystery. Or perhaps waiting for me to make a contribution. Her silence was not contented. Pregnant with something:

resentment, most likely. Of my silence. My indisputable boredom.

'I think they're lazy,' I said, making a valiant effort to be interesting or original, or perhaps simply irritating. In fact I hardly know them. Sarah and Jane. 'The girls'. Smaller, more attractive versions of their mother, dressed, like her, in faded denim jeans or skirts and striped T-shirts, always, it seemed. Never changed styles. Somewhat odd in that characteristic, come to think of it. Other women do. Chop and change. Their minds and their outfits. One day prim and proper in suits and white collars, the next gypsyish in Indian smocks and sandals.

My secretary is like that. Not that she's my personal secretary, I'm not such a significant figure in the Teddy Bums universe. I share her with three others. Travellers, like myself. Still, they all, we all, tend to refer to her as 'my secretary'. It's part of the job, really, to sound more important than one is, when dealing with clients. The habit sticks then, after work.

'Oh no they're not lazy,' Karen archetypal mother, leapt to the defence of her young.

I had known them when they were young. Truly young. Babies. I had changed their nappies and had given them the morning feed before going out. I had been a student then, doing an MA in Medieval History. A poor two had sent me scurrying into the security of Teddy Bums when Sarah was three. We needed the money. Apart from which, I needed to feel that I was a useful member of society, a parent slaving to support his little family. Even after that, although I hadn't much time to spare, I used to bring 'the girls' for walks on Saturday afternoons, in the raw forsaken countryside that lay to one edge of our suburb. I delivered long lectures on birds and trees, and the elements, subjects about which I knew absurdly little, but about which they, being so young, knew even less. At the age of five or so they outgrew me. (They both seemed to reach this age simultaneously, although Jane is in fact a year younger than Sarah.) They went to school and acquired other interests. Since then they had virtually ignored me. It was easy. I hardly ever saw them.

'Definitely not lazy. Especially not Sarah. She irons all the clothes every week, did you know that? I give her a pound for it. Did you know that?'

'No. I hadn't noticed, I must say. Would you like more wine?'

Before I had time to take the carafe old Brown Eyes was at my side, teeth aglow in the dim light. 'Madam...Sir...' He poured the bitter libation. Red house-wine. The most unappetising drink there is. Especially with Tandoori food. Beer is much better. You need the quantity and the coolness. But Karen disliked beer. And the bi-monthly visit to the 'Taj Mahal' was her treat.

'I called down to St Matilda's yesterday. I met the headmistress. Mother Gertrude, she's called. She was most interested. Thought, yes, that Sarah would certainly benefit from tuition there. She was most impressed with her marks. She wants her to come and see her sometime. She could begin after Christmas, she says. Oh, it's such a magnificent place. The gymnasium. The playing-fields. They even have a pool. Oh, she'll just love it!'

'The fees are not exactly low.'

Twelve hundred pounds a year. When we were first married we lived on considerably less than twelve hundred pounds a year. In a flat in Ranelagh. It wasn't luxurious. Or even comfortable. But it had orange walls and yellow doors and big cushions on the floor instead of chairs, and I liked it. As soon as I began to work, our expenses soared. A mortgage was immediately necessary, a car was desirable. As my salary increased so did our needs. An interior decorator became necessary, a fitted kitchen (Karen called it 'a dream kitchen') was essential, a bigger car a must. When it was all perfect, a better address was required. Now a private school, albeit a day school, would be beneficial. Life still felt the same, as far as I was concerned. The same as when I started work, that is. The same routine, the same tiredness. It was played out, partly, in more middle-class surroundings, that was all.

'Oh, well, we can manage it. If we just give up our holiday next year. I must say, I'm tired of the sun. I mean, it's pretty much the same, wherever you go, isn't it? Greece, Italy, Morocco. It's lying on the beach and burning yourself to a cinder, or it's gazing at treasure after treasure, in some hot stuffy city, or it's shopping in cool bazaars, buying stuff you don't really need, or even like after a couple of weeks. It's just not necessary. A fortnight in Kerry can be just as much fun, I'll bet. I used to love that when I was a child.'

We had been to Florence for two weeks in July. For years I had longed to go there. When I was a student, it had been a Mecca for my classmates. One had spent a summer there, selling ice-cream, another a three month term studying art, ostensibly, at least. One had emigrated to Florence as soon as the degree exams finished and never returned. I had a postcard from her once, a picture of a winding narrow street, 'I live here. Just imagine, I live in the most wonderful city in the world.' A somewhat excitable girl. She, like me, like all of us, had been a medievalist, but Florence, product of the death of the Middle Ages, meant more to us than any other place. It seemed so human. It was humanist and humane in that things happened to people there. I don't know what, precisely, but always got the impression that people fell passionately in love in Florence, or discovered their deepest selves in sudden blinding flashes of insight, or learned the secret of life. It took me fifteen years longer than it had any of my fellows to visit the city of dreams and test it. But it had not failed me. I had adored it: the streets, the palaces containing the ideal number of ideal objects, that general feeling of being in a golden section, so perfectly proportioned is everything in Florence. I had loved it but had not been entirely happy there: to cast aside my bitterness towards my way of life, my irritation at Karen, had proven beyond me, even in such ideal surroundings.

A couple came and occupied the table on my right. The girl was young, twenty-ish, with a black frizzed hairstyle and cheesecloth dress. The man was small and thin, dressed in jeans and a patched up sweater. He had a sharp nose and I disliked him on sight. Karen, I observed, glanced at the girl with a trace of emotion on her lips. They are expressive and tremble slightly when she is moved in any way. Perhaps she envied the girl, I thought, with surprise. Perhaps Karen wanted to look like that, like an ageing hippy? Her striped T-shirts, her old jeans, possibly constituted an attempt to achieve such a style. The girl had, in some mysterious manner, contrived to create a co-ordinated unmistakable 'look', whereas Karen, through timidity or lack of conviction, always managed to look sloppy, and no more.

They refused a menu from the waiter, who was a different one from ours. More sprightly, somehow. I cannot tell a Muslim from a Hindu but theirs, I would have guessed, was the former. He had a ferocity about him, even when nodding and grimacing and fawning over them in accordance with the requirements of his profession. They ordered something which took long to describe: they seemed to more or less give him the full recipe. Then they drank deep draughts of beer from tankards which they had carried with them from the bar, rather grandiosely described as a cocktail bar by the proprietors of the 'Taj Mahal'.

They began to discuss a play which they had obviously just been attending. It was called *Montaillou* and was based upon an historical study of a place of that name, in France. Soon it emerged that they had not been at the play as auditors but had actually performed in it. At least, the girl had. She had played the part of a shepherdess or a farmer's daughter or something along those lines, and he seemed to have directed, or stage-managed, or played some highly significant busy-body role behind the scenes. He talked dogmatically and fluently. She drawled whenever she got an opportunity to open her mouth, which was not often. It sounded like an extremely dull play and I resolved not to be persuaded into going to it.

'Well, I don't think I'll have dessert,' said Karen, who

had, like me, been listening to the new couple's conversation with the greatest of attention.

'No, I won't either,' I responded, returning disconsolately to my congealing chicken.

'I think I might like a liqueur, though, wouldn't you?'

'Mm. Why not?' We always had liqueurs, and we never had desserts, and she always asked.

They progressed from talking about the play to chattering of actors and other artistic personalities in their circle. Jem was down at Annaghmakerrig giving a course. He hated losing his own time and privacy but on the other hand he welcomed the contact with real people. Angie had divorced for the second time and had moved into a cottage where she was trying to weave and bring up Tasha on social welfare, since there had been some problem with the alimony. They were not sure what the problem was, but she didn't get any. I felt sorry for her. The cottage was in a rural district and was very dirty and earthy and D.H. Lawrence. The girl, our girl, our neighbour, was experiencing difficulty in finding a new contract after *Montaillou*. She was thinking of taking a break and going to Florence for a few months . . .

'We've just been there,' I said, forgetting that I was not taking part in the conversation.

The man turned to me coldly.

'Is that so?'

Karen smiled at him, embarrassed. 'He's a bit absent-minded sometimes,' she explained, patronisingly.

The girl looked at me. 'I've never been in Florence,' she said. Then they turned away from us and ate in silence for some time, to my acute pain. Our liqueurs came, a Benedictine for me and a Cointreau for Karen. We swallowed them hastily, paid and left.

It was raining. The car was parked at the railway station, five minutes walk from the 'Taj Mahal'. We walked uncomfortably through the drizzle, towards lights which glowed menacingly in the dark, with a sort of Hound of the Baskervilles effect.

At the car Karen said: 'I'll drive.' I submitted to the

indignity of the passenger seat.

She drove with an air of calm command, which usually betokened sulkiness, in her, as in many other people I knew (including myself).Past 'The Railway Arms', up the coast road, by the black featureless seascape, she maintained silence. So did I, needless to add. As we approached Dalkey and caught sight of the threatening castle which indicated the proximity of home, she turned on the cassette recorder. One of her cassettes: Simon and Garfunkel, 'Bridge Over Troubled Waters'. A tawdry hangover from her college days in the sixties. I disliked the song and the singers intensely. Always had done. At that moment, they irritated me to the point of madness.

I turned off the cassette. 'Karen, will you stop for a minute?'

She stopped the car. Was that what I had meant? Perhaps not, but since she had interpreted the order in that way, I decided to use the opportunity for what it was worth. Or some inner personality, much stronger than my true self, made such a decision.

'Karen, there's something I've got to say.' Not a very clever opening. I would have preferred to be more original. But originality in these circumstances would have been an unnecessary luxury — even though I am fond of luxuries of certain kinds under certain circumstances, this was not the time for indulgence.

'Yes,' she said. It was not original either but it was safe.

'I've got to leave you. And the children. For a while at least. I've got to find myself. Something like that.' Simon and Garfunkel would have found more elegant clichés. But I'm not gifted, verbally, and I hadn't practised or anticipated the conversation, and mainly, as I spoke these words, so harsh, so abrupt, so mad, as it seems in retrospect, and also so brave and frank and wonderful, I didn't care about rhetoric, or about anything. I felt reckless and abandoned.

Karen didn't answer. She turned her face away from me. She looked out the window, at a dark hedge.

'I'm bored with my life. You know that. You've known it for ages. I've got to find an alternative. Before it's too late.'

She continued to be silent. This forced me to keep talking, to sink in the quagmire of my ineptitude. Did she hope to make a complete fool of me, or what? Was she genuinely in a state of shock? Shocked into a state completely alien to her nature, a state of silence.

'I'll drive if you like,' I said kindly. The sooner we got home the better.

She climbed out of the car and came around to the passenger side. Within minutes we were home.

'I'll sleep in the living room, if you like.' I wanted to be considerate. The double bed we had shared until now seemed inappropriate.

'All right.' Karen's voice could only be described as expressionless. I deduced that she had switched herself off emotionally, and would react at a later stage. Or that she was possibly resting, gathering momentum before launching a really powerful offensive.

Quietly, I arranged some blankets and pillows on the sofa. I could hear Karen moving about on the floor above, going through her bedtime rituals: teeth, facecream, hair. Clothes in a heap on the floor. Bed. I knew it like the back of my hand, and could interpret every footfall correctly. The ultimate rut. But I was gratified to hear that she was behaving sensibly, and, relieved, I fell into a sound slumber. After an emotional crisis I usually sleep well.

When I awoke, golden bars of sunshine striped the carpet, and a blackbird was singing on the front lawn. Full of energy, I jumped off the sofa and skipped into the kitchen, which was all aglow with fresh morning light, the light of my new life. In celebration of the fact, I prepared a substantial breakfast — usually I just grab a coffee and run. Eggs, bacon. Tomato and toast. Percolated coffee. I placed the lot on the table, and tucked in. Before I was even half-way through, Sarah, clad in her bathrobe, which is short and pink, came in.

'Where's Mother?' she asked.

'Oh, asleep, I suppose,' I replied, offhandedly. 'Like a little bacon and eggs?'

'No she's not,' she said, crossly. 'Her bed is made. I hate eggs.'

'Hmm.' I put some tomato into my mouth, found that I didn't have the heart to swallow it, and put it surreptitiously on my plate. I ran upstairs, two steps at a time. Sarah was right. The bed either hadn't been slept in, or had been made already. There was no sign of Karen anywhere. Investigating, I discovered that her suitcase had gone. I glanced anxiously at the driveway. The car had also disappeared. 'Good God!' I cried, in horror. 'The bitch has stolen my car!'

Two weeks later, I received a short note. Karen was in Chelsea, staying with a friend (what friend?) and looking for a job. In the meantime, perhaps it would be best if the girls stayed with me. She'd be in touch.

Three months later, just before Christmas, she got in touch. A card with a picture of a glass of wine and a plum pudding outside, a few hurried lines within: she was working in a small art gallery on the King's Road, and had taken a flat in Earl's Court. It was fun. She hoped I was discovering my new self and wished me the compliments of the season.

The girls received similar cards, but theirs contained an invitation to London for the January sales, which they accepted. On their return, they had little to report. Mother was well. The flat was small and smelled of gas. Jeans were cheaper in London than in Dublin: they'd bought three new pairs apiece.

It's August now. I've just come back from Florence. Teddy Bums were generous and gave me three weeks this year, a sort of compassionate gesture, to console me for the separation which will come up in six months' time. I'd planned to do Florence really thoroughly, to absorb the atmosphere properly this time. But I only stayed for a week. It was dull, somehow. Alone.

Fulfilment

KILLINEY is the anglicisation of *Cill Inion Léinin*, the chapel of the daughter of Léinín. Who she was I do not know. Perhaps a saint like Gobnait of Cill Ghobnait. Or a princess like Isolde of Chapelizod. Perhaps she was just the daughter of a butcher, born in the Coombe, moving out to Killiney to demonstrate her upward social mobility, like many of those who live there. It is a fashionable address. An inconvenient, overcrowded, unplanned jumble of estates, possessing, nevertheless, a certain social cachet. It was that which drew me to it, first.

Some people think I came for the scenery. My house is practically on the beach. From the front room I can gaze at Bray Head, spectacular for a suburban view. The strand itself unwinds in a silver ribbon from the bathroom window. It is long and composed of coarse grains of sand which cut your feet if you walk barefoot thereon. I never do. There is no reason to do so unless you want to swim. And swimming from Killiney Strand is an activity which loses much of its appeal as soon as the hulking grey monster lurking halfway along the stretch of golden shingle is recognised for what it is: an ineffectual sewage treatment plant. Shit from Shankill, nuclear waste from Windscale, can have a dissuasive effect. On me, at least. Many people revel in it, however, and emerge from the sea, not deformed, but rarely quite the same as they were before they ventured in. Necks swell, pimples speckle peaches-and-cream, nipples invert and toes turn inward. And worse.

Killiney means much to me. I have lived there for thirteen years and would never forsake it. Not because I cherish any affection for the locality. The roads meandering drunkenly up and down the hill, the opulent villas perched like puffins on the edge of the cliff, the mean houses marshalled in regiments across the flatlands: these, in their essential lack of harmony, disturb my sense of the symmetrical, which is acute. Neither do I cling to Killiney because it provides me with congenial companions. I live in near isolation, enjoying little or no contact with my neighbours, apart from the occasional unavoidable shoulder rub with the post- or milkman. Some stalwart of the local residents' association drops the community newsletter, KRAM, through my letterbox every month. It often contains persuasive advertisements urging the reader to come to a social in the parish hall, or to join in a treasure hunt on the hill, or to demonstrate community spirit by participating in a litter drive on the strand, all such notices carefully stressing that these events will provide excellent opportunities for neighbours to meet and increase their acquaintanceship. Such temptations I have always resisted with little difficulty. It has never been my idea of fun to spear crisp bags or rack my brain in the solution of improbable clues with a stranger who coincidentally has elected to live within a mile or so of my abode. I am not a neighbourly being, not in that sense.

Killiney means everything to me, nevertheless, for one reason, and that alone: It was in Killiney that I discovered my *metier*. My vocation. What I was born to do.

I am a dog-killer.

I did not choose this way of life deliberately. When I was of an age to select a career, I was too indecisive a character to be able to deliberately single out anything, even a biscuit from a plate containing three different kinds (I used to close my eyes and trust to luck, usually with disastrous results). I was, as the technical term has it, a drifter. I drifted from job to job, from activity to activity, a scrap of flotsam on the sea of life. If you could call the confined noisy hopeless office world of Dublin a sea, or life. First I worked for the Corporation, which was a bit like working for the Russian civil service before the Revolution (or perhaps even after, but one doesn't know that experience so intimately). My duties consisted, for the most part, in writing addresses on envelopes, for the least, in dealing with telephone queries from a mystified but cantankerous public. After a destructive eighteen months, I sacrificed my security and pension and studied electronics for a year, at a tech. Then I worked with a computer company for six months, until I was made redundant. Then I washed dishes in a German café in Capel Street, where, incidentally, I picked up a great deal of my employers' language as well as much other information which I have since found very useful. Then, at long last I got what I considered my great break. I was given a job as a folklore collector by a museum in Dublin. I was supplied with a tape-recorder and camera, and every day I walked around the city and environs ferreting out likely informants. When I had tracked them down, I interviewed them, interrogating them on a wide variety of topics loosely related to traditional belief and practice, with the aid of an easy-to-follow guide book. It was a fascinating and rewarding task, entirely suited to my skills and disposition. It cultivated in me a taste for adventure, exploration and, above all, absolute freedom to order my days without deference to the will of an authoritative, pettifogging bureaucracy. These tastes, once realised, developed in strength and persistence, so that liberty soon became an imperative for survival as far as I was concerned. When my collecting job finished, as it did inevitably and all too soon, I was left nursing the burden of the knowledge that I could never again return to the slavery of a nine-to-five position, which indignity I had endured for seven long years before my break.

The question was, what should I do instead? Killiney gave me the answer. I had officially been resident there for two years before my collecting job collapsed. My enthusiasm for my work had been such, however, that I had hitherto paid little attention to my surroundings, frequently, indeed, not returning home at night, but bedding down in the flat of a colleague, or in the home of one of the friendly folk who provided me with the stuff of my occupation. But, even in that state of almost total apathy to environmental hazards, it had often struck me that Killiney suffered from unusually severe infestation by the canine species in all its varieties, too numerous to mention and in any case not known to me by name, except for some of the more common forms, such as Golden Labrador or Cocker Spaniel. I had once been bitten by a lean and hungry Alsatian belonging to some itinerants who camped, with my full approval (not that they asked for it, or required it) on an undeveloped site at the end of my lane. I had had to go to St Michael's for a tetanus injection, which had been administered by an aggressive nurse wearing steel-rimmed spectacles. On another occasion, a minute Pekinese, a breed which I particularly distrust, scraped the skin off the heel of an expensive shoe I had just purchased. Apart from these extreme incidents, every night that I spent in Killiney was filled with the mournful howling of dogs. Any walk taken in the neighbourhood was spoiled by the effort of fighting my fear of being bitten, of planning, futilely, itineraries which would take me out of the beasts' range, or of physically chasing off the ever-encroaching packs of curs.

When I had finished collecting folklore and had begun to live in Killiney almost constantly, it soon became apparent to me that the dog problem was rendering life unbearable: not only my life, but everyone else's as well.

My work as a folklore collector had not only awoken in me a healthy desire to master my own experience. It had imbued me with what can best be described as an altruistic streak. I wanted to improve the existence of others, too. In short, I was burning with ambition to be of service to mankind.

Killiney showed me the way.

My first dog-killing was fortuitous. I was walking home from the station one evening, having spent a particularly wearisome day trying to get a week's supply of food for four pounds, followed by an attempt to obtain an admission card to the National Library, where I had hoped to improve my mind with some classical reading while I considered my future. Both efforts had been fruitless. Lightly laden with two sliced pans, two tins of baked beans and a pound of liver, I had meandered up Kildare Street, the consciousness of impending starvation slowing my footsteps. My entrance to the Library was first blocked by a stern official in a blue suit, who accused me of trying to force entry without a reader's ticket, and thoroughly investigated the contents of my plastic bag. He suspected it of containing a bomb, he explained afterwards. He then directed me to the office of an even sterner official with startling blue hair who informed me in no uncertain terms that the National Library had no accommodation to spare for the likes of me. My pleas lasted the best part of an hour, but were all in vain. The more I reasoned, the stronger grew his opposition. Finally I left, strolling through the reading room on my way out. The porter in the hall did not check my bag, which I found convenient, since I had tucked into it the second volume of Plummer's *Lives of the Saints*, a work now exceedingly difficult to procure honestly but a handsome set of which adorned the library's open-access shelves. I resolved to return at my earliest opportunity to steal the remaining volumes, with the intention of making them available to an antiquarian bookseller just around the corner of Kildare Street.

I refreshed myself after the ordeal with a glass of lager

in a nearby hotel, and then used my last fifty pence in the purchase of a ticket to Killiney Station. I was obliged to endure the journey in a vertical position, since I had stupidly elected to travel on the five-fifteen, the most crowded train in Ireland. My state of mind was, therefore, far from tranquil or positive when, half way down Station Road, a dog, something like a collie but with a terrier's nose, dashed across my path and attempted to grab my raincoat in his mawful of bared teeth. I lowered my umbrella before you could say Jack Robinson and hammered him on the skull. To my intense relief he immediately released his vice-like grip and lay, subdued, at my toes. I stared at his immobile body for a moment or two, enjoying a vigorous sensation of triumph. I waited, patiently, for the beast to struggle to his paws and slink furtively away, tail demurely tucked between legs, aware of who was master. A minute passed and he did not stir. The smile which had played on my lips receded. Thirty more seconds elapsed. He continued to lie prostrate on the concrete path. Not a whimper passed his lips. I bent down and touched his hairy back, somewhat gingerly. It was warm to my fingers, but I felt uneasy. There was an unearthly stillness in the texture of the fur. I turned his head over and his eyes bored into mine. Round and lifeless, rolling in their sockets. Aghast, I sprang to my feet. The cooling lump of dog meat on the path was dead, and I had killed it! Never until that moment had I murdered a fly.

Fortunately, my keen instinct for survival warned me that there was no time to be lost in foolish lamenting over spilt milk. The immediate necessity was to dispose of the dog with maximum haste and secrecy. Observing that all was quiet on the road, not a soul in sight, I emptied my plastic bag of its contents and hid them under a bush. In their place I put the deceased animal, intending to carry him home and give him a decent funeral: I could simply not run the risk of being asked to financially compensate some distraught pet owner. The dog appeared to be a valueless mongrel but you never know. Sometimes it is precisely the ugliest specimens who turn out to have pedigrees as long as your arm. I knew of a charming spot near the sewage-plant where my victim would rest in eternal peace, since no one, human or canine, ever ventured there, for obvious reasons.

I walked home from what I preferred to regard as the scene of the accident, and placed the victim on the kitchen floor. Then I returned to the black spot to collect my groceries. They, however, were not to be found. Some cruel villain had stolen them. There goes dindins for five days, I thought, glumly. How could I survive without food until dole day, a whole week off? Hunger reared its ugly head, not for the first time during my spell of unemployment.

Strolling homewards, I noticed torn slices of bread, scraps of bloodied butcher's paper, in short, the debris of my groceries, scattered at intervals along the road. About a hundred yards from where the tragedy had occurred a large ugly dog relaxed in the shadow of a tree, langorously devouring the last of the liver. Horrible brute! I thought, wishing I had my umbrella with me, in order to give him a well-deserved whack. But it had stopped raining and my weapon was in its teak stand in my little hall.

Back in the cottage, I sat in the living room and stared vacantly at Bray Head. It was black and awe-inspiring against the grey evening sky, but it afforded me no refreshment. My stomach rumbled, a dead dog lay on my kitchen floor awaiting burial, and, once again, rain bucketed forth from the heavens, preventing all action. I hadn't a single penny in my purse. After a dreary hour of staring, I went to bed, supping on a drink of water, the quality of which was far from high.

Morning dawned bright and sunny, lifting my spirits momentarily. My breakfast of stale oats and cold water effected a deterioration of mood, restoring me to a realisation of my undesirable predicament. The eyes of the dog, clear blue, were wide open and seemed to follow every move I made. If I'd had two pennies I would have placed them on those Mona Lisa orbs and shut them for once and for all (it was a trick traditionally used in the preparation of the dead for burial, as my old friends in the Liberties had often told me). As I rinsed my bowl in the earthenware sink, it occurred to me, suddenly, like a bolt out of the sky, that I was not, after all, going to cart the heavy dog all the way down to the sewage plant, nervously avoiding encounters with morning strollers. I was not going to cart him anywhere at all. I was going to eat him.

In my work as a folklore collector, I had spent two months investigating a particular genre of tale known professionally as the modern legend. Modern legends are stories which concern strange or horrifying or hilariously amusing events, and circulate as the truth in contemporary society. An example is the story of the theatre tickets. A man finds that his car is missing from its usual parking place. He reports the theft to the police, but a day later the car has been returned. Pinned to the windscreen is a note of apology, and two tickets for a theatre show that night, as a token of amendment. The car owner and his wife use the tickets, and return at midnight to find that their house has been burgled. Another example is 'The Surprise Birthday Party'. A man wakes on his birthday to find that he has received no cards or greetings whatsoever. He goes to work and, at lunchtime, his secretary invites him to accompany her to her flat for lunch. He accepts the invitation with alacrity, and they proceed to her apartment. She leaves him in the living room and entering the bedroom, says she will be back in a minute. He uses the opportunity to undress, and is sitting on the sofa, completely naked, when the bedroom door bursts open and his wife, children, neighbours and colleagues leap into the room singing 'Happy Birthday to You'. In the course of my wanderings in Dublin I had learned that the best-known legend, amounting really to little more than belief, reported the use of dog as food in Chinese restaurants. Alsatian Kung Fu, Sweet and Sour Terrier, Collie Curry, were familiar names to me. It had taken only a trifle of investigation to discover that it was untrue that the Chinese served dog in their Irish outlets, but that in China and other parts of Asia, dog was consumed as a normal part of the diet.

I got out my carving-knife (my mother had given it to me as a house-warming present when I moved to the cottage: it is a long sharp knife with a bone handle, an antique, she told me) and flayed the animal. It was not easy, but neither was it as difficult as it may sound. In a matter of an hour or so the soft brown skin, dripping, it must be admitted, with soft wet blood, lay on a wad of newspaper on the floor. Then I sliced meat off the trunk of the dog: its legs were fragile and skinny and would be good for nothing but stock. Within half an hour, I had removed all edible flesh from the carcass (I had long ceased to think of it as a corpse). I carried the remains out to the yard and pondered how best to dispose of them. First I considered burning, but decided that the smell of roasting flesh might carry to my unknown neighbours and arouse anxiety among them. I secondly contemplated dumping them into the adjacent ocean. This thought developed rapidly into a better plan. I would walk to the sewage-plant where I had first considered burying the total animal, and throw what remained of him into the cesspool, which was open to the public. The body would be processed with the effluent from Shankill and whatever else went into the stinking hole, and leave no trace to be discovered, now or ever. The plan seemed so foolproof that I immediately felt happier than I had at any stage of my life since my terrible encounter with the keepers of the national literature some twenty hours earlier.

It worked like a dream. No one observed me as I plodded along the uncomfortable shingle towards the plant. No one observed me climb to the edge of the cesspool, and no one observed me tip the sack of bones into it. Coming home, sauntering along the tide line, now and then running out to avoid a brazen wave, I met a man leading a red setter, and bade him a cheery 'Good morning'. He smiled genially in response. No trace of knowledge or malice marked his weather-beaten countenance. I had been undetected.

I made a curry of the meat for Saturday's dinner: I had some spices in my cupboard, relics from more affluent days, as well as a cup of brown rice, which I prefer to the white: it is so much better for the digestion. The meal was superb: aromatic, tender, of a delicacy which I had never sampled before in the take-aways of Blackrock, Dun Laoghaire or even China, which I had visited as a student on a package trip. I had some leftover curry for Sunday's lunch (it tasted even better then) and two hefty cutlets for tea on the Sabbath. I had not eaten so well in several months.

The skin of the dog lay in my yard over the weekend. The blood dried off and the pelt seemed to be curing itself naturally. I cut off the straggly corners where the legs and tail protruded. I always hate those bits of animal skins, even on sheepskins. They seem so ostentatious. As if one were giving proof that the skin were real and not spun-nylon. I laid my genuine pelt in front of the fireplace. It looked shaggy, warm and inviting. I decided that I would refer to it in future conversations, even those which were conducted exclusively in my own company, (which accounted for most), as my antelope, received from a friend who hunted in Gambia, where, I vaguely recalled, antelope still survived in sufficient numbers to be hunted. My friend visited Africa every spring, I'd decided, when the antelope were small.

One thing led to another. My natural antipathy to the canine species, my diagnosis of Killiney's main problem as the dog problem, my urgent need for lucrative entrepreneurial employment, all conspired to persuade me that dog-killing would be my next job. I plunged into it with my whole heart. It was so easy, after all, to find prey. Indeed, it usually found me, snapping and yelping at my feet whenever I ventured out of the house. It was a simple matter to remember to carry my large umbrella, bought, in any case, as a weapon, and to batter any nosy beast on the head, on the right spot just above the temple (death was invariably instant and painless). I always carried a big shopping bag on my hunting expeditions, and suffered few setbacks in transporting carcasses from strand, street or railway to my home.

My methods of disposing of the products of my enterprise varied and expanded in variety as time passed. Initially basing my plans on the knowledge I had acquired as a folklore collector, I offered the flesh, neatly packaged in plastic cling-foil, to restaurants, at prices which were attractively but not suspiciously low. I did not, of course, approach Chinese or Indonesian restaurants. The owners would have immediately recognised my wares for what they were, and who knows what their reactions would be. Never trust a foreigner. No, I circulated the more exclusive native establishments, the cosy wee bistros with which the southern coastline of Dublin is so liberally peppered. I had, on the rare occasions when I had treated myself to a repast at 'The Spotted Dog' or 'The Pavlovian Rat', to name a couple of the better establishments, noted that they served food which was spiced and sauced to such a degree that its basic ingredients, no doubt of the best quality, were totally unrecognisable. They might as well have served *Rat à la Provencale,* or *Cat Bourguignon,* for all the evidence of veal or beef one could detect in either. The inhabitants of South Dublin, reared for the most part in primitive Ireland (i.e. not South Dublin) know nothing about food. All through their formative years they are fed on the Irish housekeeping tradition, and nothing else. Their mothers, bursting with pride about their home cooking, can concoct at best soda bread (the most tasteless, unhealthy bread imaginable), mixed grills, and boiled chicken. The natural reaction after such a diet is to crave the most elaborate messes of marjoram, tarragon, garlic, cream cheese, tomatoes, wine, ginger, and turmeric, all rolled into one cosmopolitan topping for pork masquerading as veal or monkfish doing duty for prawns. This taste is well catered for in every suburban village, if they can be called villages, those outcrops of shops and pubs and chapels which stud the concrete jungle from

Bray to Booterstown. The northern Dubliner, at least while he stays on his own side of the river, probably still relies on his native cuisine, that is, coddle. I knew a man in the Corporation from Finglas West who always cooked coddle for lunch. He put it on at eleven o'clock at his tea-break and took it off at one, when it was done to a turn. He gave me a saucerful once. Delicious!

The reception I received at first from the proprietors and chefs of my local *trattoria* was not enthusiastic. It was on the whole suspicious. Where had I got the meat? Did I have identification? And so on.

It was not hard to procure an identity card. What is identification, after all? Just a card stating that you are who you claim to be. Having to create cards, however, prompted me to use several aliases, something which would never have occurred to me had I not been asked for identification in the first place.

As to explaining the provenance of the meat, I had, prior to my very first visit to the manager of a cosy kitchen in Dalkey, fabricated my story. The meat, I had decided was not antelope, but wild goat, imported from the North, where wild goats abound in the hills of Antrim and Tyrone. I had a partner in Crossmaglen who procured the meat for me from local lads, target practising in the mountainy regions. It was tasty and healthy, perfect for Cordon Bleu cookery. Indeed, I added, Swiss chefs prized goats above any other viand. The belief that it was stringy and tough was ill-founded. I would give the *restaurateur* a sample batch, free, for testing.

This tale, in conjunction with the identity card, worked. It was the bit about the North which added the final touch of plausibility to my explanation. Anything could happen in the North, in the view of Dublin burghers. They had heard of smuggled TV s and refrigerators, smuggled pigs and cattle. Why not smuggled goat?

To cut a long story short, within six months I was regularly supplying twenty restaurants with dog meat and making a tidy profit. I continued to dump the denuded carcasses in the cesspool, but found that I was having a problem with the increasing heap of skins in my back yard: yellow, black, brown and red, they lay there in a multi-coloured pile. I had carpeted my living room with them, and very fine it looked, but I did not want my whole house covered with reminders of my trade, and, even had I wanted it, I would have encountered a problem sooner or later.

After much deliberation I decided to shave the dog skins and keep the hairs. The leftover skin I would, perhaps, at some future stage, sew into handbags, belts and other fancy leather goods. For the present, I contented myself with the purchase of forty yards of yellow cotton, and proceeded to make beanbags and cushions which I stuffed with dog hair. I opened a stall in a street market in town where I would not be recognised as the goat importer, and most Saturdays and Sundays I could be found there vending my wares to a receptive public: my products were cheaper, softer and more hard-wearing than anyone else's.

Time went on, as it does, and I became more and more comfortable financially, and more and more fulfilled as a human being. I developed my hunting technique, advancing from the simple umbrella to the more complicated sling, which, of course, had the advantage of being able to kill from a distance, and on to the even more complex pop-gun. I began to travel the length and breadth of Dublin, realising that if I depleted the canine population of Killiney too much and too quickly someone would become anxious and interfere. As luck would have it, nobody at all seemed to notice what was happening, although the community benefitted in no uncertain measure.

Good fortune is never limitless, and I was caught at last. It happened as I strolled along Dollymount Strand, popgun in pocket, car parked nearby, stalking a large English Sheepdog. Normally I did not touch English

Sheepdogs or other expensive models with a ten-foot pole, but this one seemed to be very much alone. It had an abandoned look in its shaggy fringes and the lope of its melancholy feet spoke of endless deprivation. I felt it would be a kindness to take the animal out of its misery, and took a shot from a distance of fifty yards. The beast toppled and fell. Immediately, a man grabbed my shoulders. He was young over six feet tall, and broad-shouldered. I did not struggle.

'I saw what you just did,' he said. He had an American accent and whined. 'You just shot my dawg!'

'Why, yes, I did,' I said.

'You can even stand there and admit it to my face!'

'Of course I can admit it. Why shouldn't I admit it? It was a complete mistake! Please accept my heartfelt apologies.'

'Aw! Sure it was a mistake! I saw you. You took aim and fired at him. My dawg!'

'I was trying to shoot that buoy over there,' I said, pointing at one of those plastery-looking life-savers in a wooden box which was, luckily enough, situated close to where the dog had fallen.

'I'm taking you to the police. Tell them your story if you like.'

He ushered me along the beach towards a Renault 12, red in colour, pausing on the way to examine the taxation disc on my windscreen. Then he drove rapidly down to the Bull Wall, across the bridge and to Clontarf barracks.

'You won't believe what I'm going to tell you,' he said to the sergeant, who was sitting beside a gas fire reading the *News of the World.*

'Well?' said the sergeant, with a great show of patience. His name, I noticed from a sign on the desk, was Sergeant Byrne. An unusual name for a Dublin guard.

'This broad here . . .' he indicated me with a flick of his shoulder '. . . shot my dawg.'

'What?' Sergeant Byrne looked up from his paper in some surprise.

'She shot my dawg. With a shotgun.'

'What is your name?' Sergeant Byrne asked me. I handed him one of my identity cards. *Imelda Byrne, 10 Dundela Park, Sandycove,* it stated.

'Do you have a gun licence?'

'No. It's a toy gun.'

'Let me see it.'

I showed him my pop-gun. It is a toy gun. It shoots wooden pellets. The trick is to aim at the temple.

'Well, well,' said the sergeant, 'and why did you shoot this man's dog?'

'It was a mistake. I was target practising. I play golf, you see, and someone told me it would be good training for the eye to shoot at targets with a pop-gun.'

'I saw her aim at my dawg.'

'Yes, yes, well,' said the sergeant, 'we'll hold her for questioning. You can press charges, if you like. Fill in this and post it to us as soon as possible.' He handed the American a form.

The American departed, muttering under his breath. The sergeant sat, re-opened his paper and looked at me quizzically.

'Target practising is an odd sport for a lady to carry out on a Sunday afternoon. Can't you find a healthier way of passing the time?'

'I usually play golf.'

'Oh, yes, yes. Where do you play?'

'Newlands.'

'Oh, yes, yes. Hard to get into these days, isn't it? I play a bit of golf myself, you know. Up at Howth, usually. Very hard to get into a good club.'

'Yes.'

'Hm. So you shot this dog, did you? Haha! Well, to tell you the truth, the more dogs get shot, the better life will be in this neighbourhood. I'm moidhered with them and with people's complaints about them. What can I do? I'm only human. Now, be off with you.'

I collected my car from the beach and drove home. It was a great relief to me to know that what my heart has always told me was true: right and might were on my side. I was fighting the good fight.

After my ordeal on Bull Island, I decided to relax for at least one evening. Normally my Sunday nights were absorbed in account-keeping, doing the books, as the phrase has it, for the week. But on this particular Sunday I lit a fire in the drawing room and settled down to watch a video: I had a complete set of Bergman movies that I had not watched before. I adore Bergman. The film I selected was *Face to Face*, a slow-moving study of a psychiatrist and her relationship with her daughter, patients, husband, lovers, and others. I was just getting involved in it when my door-knocker sounded. A rare, almost unique, occurrence. I smelt danger immediately but had no option but to open it, since the blue glow of my living room would have indicated to anyone that I was in, glued to the box. At the door were two policemen, who asked me if I were Jane O'Toole. Shocked, I admitted that I was. They produced a warrant for my arrest.

I got six months. The judge said it was as much as he could impose although he heartily wished he could condemn me to a life of hard labour. My offence, he said, in a long tedious monologue at the end of my three-day trial, was the most heinous he had encountered in his life. I had been responsible, he said, for the killing of at least a thousand dogs (in fact, twice that). Responsible dogs. The beloved pets of the citizens of Dublin.

Now I am sitting in Mountjoy in the female wing, engaged in writing an autobiographical novel. Public sympathy for my crusade against the dogs is expressed by a flood of letters from people who have, in one way or another, been molested by them. Even the warders, a tough and unemotional crew, express concern for the fact that several hundred dogs roam the area within half a mile radius of the prison and threaten them every time they leave for a walk or to go home.

I am comfortable in prison and happy with the degree of freedom which I am allowed. I do not have to work and the only constraints are physical: I am not allowed outside the high walls which surround the penitentiary. Inside, I may do as I wish. I am not as happy as I was when enjoying my career as a dog-killer, but I am happier than I have been in many of my other jobs. I find fulfilment of a kind in writing down my account of my life's experiences and struggle for freedom. More than one publisher has expressed interest in my project, which has already received considerable publicity in the media. According to some agents, I stand to score a huge success with the book. It will, they explain, be a matter of 'hype', and already it has been hyped to a much greater extent than any author would wish, and all for free. I could, taking into account the possibilities of film rights, translations, and so on, make at least a hundred thousand. And it will, like all my previous profits, be tax-free.